SKYSHAKER

THE GREAT IRON WAR - BOOK THREE

SKYSHAKER

DEAN F. WILSON

Cover illustration by Duy Phan

First Edition 2015

ISBN 978-1-909356-13-9

Published by Dioscuri Press
Dublin, Ireland

www.dioscuripress.com
enquiries@dioscuripress.com

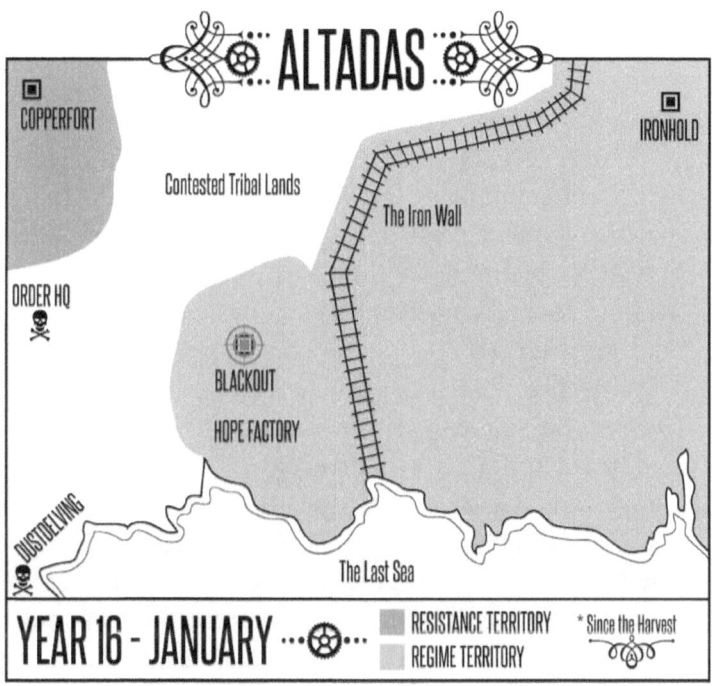

ALTADAS

COPPERFORT

IRONHOLD

Contested Tribal Lands

The Iron Wall

ORDER HQ

BLACKOUT

HOPE FACTORY

DUSTDELVING

The Last Sea

YEAR 16 - JANUARY

RESISTANCE TERRITORY
REGIME TERRITORY

* Since the Harvest

THE GREAT IRON WAR

In the world of Altadas, in the year 1888 of the Second Era, women everywhere dreamed of a coming desert. Those who were already pregnant miscarried, and those who became pregnant did not give birth to human children. An invasion had begun.

The newborns had no horns or marks, and so they were loved and reared like all the others. It would take time before anyone realised what they really were, before anyone would call them demons.

These events were marked by the arrival of strangers claiming to be from a distant land. The people of Altadas called them Pilgrims, but they did not know just how far they had come, nor by what strange doors they had entered, nor exactly what they had come for.

The first Pilgrims were scouts, but subsequent waves were soldiers, sent by a man who would later call himself the Iron Emperor. He promised his people iron. He gave them war instead.

They called that year the Harvest, and it became the first year of a new, darker calendar. Sand swept through the great chasms in the sky from where the demons came, the dust of a world that they had dried up. Ahead of the landships went great sandstorms, until the green grasses became an endless red desert.

In Altadas, steam powers industry, but iron powers war. The abundant metal, idolised by the invaders, and depleted in their home world, became a beacon to the demons, and was the foundation upon which they would build their new civilisation. They called themselves the Iron Empire. Their enemies simply called them the Regime.

As war began in the east, few among the Resistance knew that their own children were not really theirs. The invaders had mastered a magical technique to control the birth channels of a people they desired to conquer. Thus with one hand they would wield might, and with the other they would use guile, infiltrating and eradicating their enemies, anyone who would dare defy the Iron Emperor, who had brought his people to this promised land.

Yet iron is more to the demons than just a metal. When broken down into its basic elements, it provides the key ingredient of the necessary sustenance of the invaders. To some it is a drug. To them, symbolising everything they were promised, and everything they were leaving behind, it is Hope.

As one civilisation crumbled, and a new empire was founded on its remains, there were some who refused to live out their last days under the iron grip of their new ruler. They made a promise of their own: to fight, with everything they had, for the fate of humanity.

Thus began the Great Iron War.

CONTENTS

Chapter

Chapter One

OF WIND AND WIRE

The airship ascended into the heavens, vacated by any angels who might have dwelt there in ages past, and the crew aboard the vessel looked down at the vast sea below them, and to the vaster desert ahead of them, gradually vacated by men. The demons who now resided there might be monstrous when faced upon the ground, but from the heights of the clouds they looked smaller than ants, and many aboard the Skyshaker felt that they might be just as easily crushed.

Rommond locked himself in his new quarters, which were smaller than those on the Lifemaker, which were in turn smaller than those at Dustdelving. It seemed that the longer the war waged on, the smaller his room became. One day it might just be big enough to sleep in, six feet deep beneath the reddest sands. His new room was not decorated with paintings or given character by books. It was bland, almost mechanical, and it was there that he plotted and planned, winding up the springs of his mind, that he might unleash them with greater force upon the enemy.

"I guess he's not coming out," Jacob said to

Taberah, who leaned against the railing of the airship, her fiery hair flailing in the wind. They were never so happy to feel fresh air upon their skin.

The Skyshaker had two modes: *cruising*, where the gondola, which housed the crew and cargo, could hang from wires and chains from the massive cigar-shaped balloon known as the envelope; or *crusading*, where the gondola was pulled up until it docked with the balloon, allowing the vessel to be pressurised with oxygen tanks, and granting the captain the freedom to elevate the airship to even greater heights. One mode was designed for peace; the other was made for war.

Yet though the Great Iron War showed no signs of ending, most of the crew enjoyed this brief respite as the Skyshaker drifted through the air, propelled by a large steam vent at the rear, and a propeller made into the gondola, and guided by a massive tail-fin, which was turned this way and that with ropes and cogs.

"Perhaps you should go see that he's okay," Jacob suggested to Taberah, who was periodically glancing at the cabin that Rommond had sealed himself in.

"I doubt he'd want me to," she replied.

"Your relationship with him is odd," Jacob remarked, not that his was any better.

"Sometimes we want different things."

"Sometimes you want the same thing," Jacob said. "Wasn't that the original problem?"

If glares had force, she would have pushed him overboard. "Well, he didn't want you involved with us. Maybe I'm coming 'round to that point of view."

Jacob gently tapped her bulging belly. "A bit late for that."

* * *

The Last Sea was far below them, and far below it was the ruined hulk of the Lifemaker. As Jacob watched the crashing waves, he could not help but think of those who went down with that leviathan of a submarine; he thought of Alson, who died as she lived, and Cala, who found death just as exciting as life.

Jacob noticed that every so often his hands trembled. He grabbed the rail more tightly. He still felt a little off since his encounter with Cala, and her forcing him to consume Hope. He was not sure if it was just that his nerves were rattled, or if the drug still pumped through his veins.

Luckily, Doctor Mudro was not hard to find, with a perpetual halo of smoke around him. He stayed on the top deck, where he could enjoy smoking the leaf more freely. Jacob called him aside, and the smoke trailed behind the doctor like ethereal wings.

"Can I get some more of that Greenshield?" Jacob asked, and he thought he sounded a little too eager, a little too desperate. He could almost hear his voice more clearly, and he did not like it.

"Oh no," Mudro said, "I couldn't do that. Greenshield can become just as addictive as Hope itself. I gave you the maximum dose. You'd need at least a week before it's out of your system."

"I'm finding it hard to concentrate."

"That's natural."

"This isn't natural," Jacob said. "I feel on edge."

"You've got to let it work its way out of its own accord. You can't rush that process."

"How long will it take?"

"Depends on the person. A few days. A week. Sometimes a month. It depends on how strong your willpower is."

"And that's the same when going cold turkey?"

"There's no other way to do it," Mudro said. "There's no magic spell to make the lust for Hope go away."

"Do me a favour," Jacob replied. "And keep this between us."

"And the boy."

"And Whistler, yeah. I wish he hadn't seen me like this."

"I wish *I* hadn't," Mudro said. "I've seen enough Hope addicts in my time. They line the streets of Blackout. I could make the statue of Mabraldan invisible, but I can't make those addicts disappear."

"Well, that won't be me."

"Let's hope not. You've got to have a reason to fight through it. A reason to live."

"You mean, I've got to have what the others don't," Jacob said. "Real hope."

"And do you?"

Jacob took some time to respond. He saw Taberah leaning against the rail, edging closer to where Whistler stood, staring out at the clouds that roamed with them. Jacob smiled. "Yeah," he said. "Yeah, I do."

The sea still simmered below them, and the sky seemed to open up even more above and around them. The Skyshaker kept at a steady height, but the shifting clouds made it seem like the heavens were always changing, making way for this royal barge, this vessel bought with Treasury loans, heading straight for the Treasury's own haven: Blackout.

Jacob paid little attention to that objective. Perhaps it was the change in air pressure, but he felt frequently nauseous, as if he was having his own kind of morning sickness. He tried to blame it on the breeze, on the creaking deck, even on Karlsif's food. He did not want to think about blaming it on the drug.

Whistler strutted up to him and hung his arms over the rail. He clearly did not have any fear of heights. In some ways, he looked more at ease, more at home, in the sky.

"Hello there, bunk-buddy," the boy said, nudging Jacob and greeting him with a grin. Everyone, bar a select elite, were sharing bunks, and almost sharing the same bed, given how cramped the conditions were. Whistler had traded his bunk with another crewman in order to pester Jacob a little more. Unsurprisingly, with his love of heights, he got the top bunk. Unsurprisingly for Jacob, with where he felt in the food chain, he got the bottom.

"Don't the clouds look funny?" Whistler suggested. He pointed to one of them. "Doesn't that one look like a horse? Maybe we fly, and the clouds gallop."

Jacob crouched down near the rail. "Yeah, an interesting thought."

"Are you okay?" Whistler asked.

"Yeah," Jacob said, clutching his stomach. Sweat formed on his brow, as if there was a little galloping cloud there, dropping down a steady stream of rain.

"You don't look okay."

"Well … I guess I've been better."

"Have you been worse?"

Jacob chuckled. "Yes, I've been worse. Half my hangovers were worse than this." *They might have been worse*, he thought, *but they didn't last this long*.

"She was crazy," Whistler said, with a tremble in his voice to match the tremble in Jacob's hands.

"Yeah, she was," Jacob acknowledged. "She's gone now though."

"For good?"

Jacob thought about Cala locked inside the Lifemaker as it descended for a final time into the deeps. He did not know how long the oxygen would last. She might have regretted sabotaging the air tanks then. Yet he knew that she did not care for regrets. He was not sure what she cared about. Perhaps nothing at all.

"For good," he said in time, wishing he had not delayed, thinking that his pause might in some way give Cala that extra gulp of air. Who knew what damage she could do with just a single breath?

"And you?" Whistler asked.

"And I what?"

"Is she gone from you for good?"

"She's just a memory now."

"What about … the Hope?"

"Just another memory."

"A bad one."

"Yes," Jacob said with a sigh. "A bad one. A bad trip."

"Well, I'm glad it's over," Whistler said, hanging back over the rail, his faded cap almost slipping from his tangled mop of red and brown, like fire and earth mingled in a messy frame.

Jacob forced a smile and placed one of his shaking hands into his pocket, to hide it from Whistler's eyes, and to hide it from his own. He felt the handful of coils there. Five of them. Just five. In the frenzy to escape the Lifemaker, and with Hope coursing through his veins, clouding his mind, he had left behind his comforting crate, his well-earned fortune. As his trembling fingers toyed with the coils in his pocket, he could not help but wonder if he had abandoned one addiction, only to find another.

Chapter Two

GUNS AND GADGETS

The Skyshaker was a much smaller vessel than the Lifemaker, but it was just as ornate. When the engineers waited for essential parts, Rommond turned them into artists, giving the airship its many flourishes, which were as much an affront to the Regime as Rommond's own survival, for he taunted them with culture. They would not just see the barrel of a gun—they would see a golden barrel, with swirls and floral motifs, and they would know that art did not weaken the people, as they claimed in their many sermons, but that it strengthened them.

Jacob wandered the ship, peeping his head through open doors, being hunted out of parts of the vessel he was not supposed to be in. It was just as much a maze as the submarine was. Jacob wondered if Rommond asked for that as a feature, to make it harder for an enemy to take over, or harder for a troublemaker to explore.

Jacob was in awe when he saw the engine room, with its many great furnaces, twice the height of man, with many times the heat. Boulder was there, shovelling piles of coal into the fire, feeding it, nursing it, yet never wholly taming it. The flames spat and licked, singeing Boulder's already well-singed clothing, tasting him. The sweat poured from him, as it always did, and he hurried back and forth, a perpetual worker, toiling when others rested from their toils.

"Need a hand?" Jacob asked.

"Always," Boulder replied, wiping his brow with his oil-soaked handkerchief.

Jacob grabbed a shovel and began loading up one of the starving furnaces, which gobbled up the little black nuggets and belched out its industrial fumes—the ugly unseen core of the otherwise pretty vessel.

"So, I guess this is how we fly," Jacob remarked.

"The balloons make us float, laddie, but this fuels the propellers and the sail."

"Why didn't you use diesel like the Lifemaker? It'd save all this work."

"We would've if we could've," Boulder replied, wiping soot on his shirt, which could not wholly contain his rotund form. "That there," he said, pointing the blackened handle of his shovel to the largest furnace, "is what makes us our steam. And steam's goin' out o' fashion, mark my words. But diesel's new, and what's new's what everybody craves. It's a kind of Hope to us engineers, so it is. The Regime controls most of the oil wells now, but they haven't made much use of 'em, thank God. They don't have the brains like Brooklyn. The General got his supplies from the biker gangs that roam Altadas. Paid a pretty penny for 'em too, as those bikers'd rather keep that stuff for themselves, so they would. He put almost all of it on the Lifemaker, because it guzzled diesel like this furnace here guzzles coal. He needed it down there, and some of us thought we might be down there for good, that we'd have to come up only to restock and refuel. The Hopebreaker's the same. Diesel engine. That's what makes it pack a punch, but our supplies are low, and Rommond wants to keep his landship in service. So when it came to finishin' off the Skyshaker, we knew we couldn't go with diesel engines. It was back to good old-fashioned steam. The old reliables, as they say."

He wiped his brow again, as if talking was just as much work. He left it just as grimy as it was before, replacing one oil with another.

"I guess we all run on steam," Jacob mused. "Food for fuel."

Boulder patted his beer belly, and his enormous sideburns quivered as he chuckled. "I prefer me some ale."

They worked for another hour, before Boulder shared a beer with him. He was a jovial man, devoted to his work, and when he was not working, he was devoted to his drink. He quaffed it like the furnaces gulped down coal, and he stole himself away from his swill only long enough for a hearty, chesty laugh. It was almost a sin for such a friendly persona to be locked away, mostly alone, in the bowels of the ship, but he never complained about it. The machinery was all the company he needed, and from what Jacob had seen, there was enough of it to befriend the entire crew.

As the beer flowed freely, and Boulder topped up the furnace between each swig, the engineer began to grow a little tipsy, and was a lot more loose-lipped than he was before. The topic soon focused on Brooklyn, who appeared to have Boulder's eternal admiration. It seemed that he was constantly looking to raise a glass to him, but could only raise it to his ghost.

"You should've seen 'im, Jacob," Boulder said with a sigh. "When he got workin' on a new vehicle, he was a wonder to behold. You'd be talkin' to him, and he'd pause, as if he heard another voice, and he'd be compelled to begin work, no matter if he was tired or hungry. No one gave him orders. The machines did that. Iron was his master."

"I wish I'd met him," Jacob said.

"Rommond used to watch him at work until all hours," Boulder continued, lost in his soliloquy. "I'd come in late to tidy up, or come in early to get things ready, and Rommond would be there, watchin' with the admiration that we all felt. They had a special kind of love. It was like a nut and bolt. Made for each other, so they were. Together they made things happen. We're only alive this long because of them. I owe my freedom and my life to them. In many ways, we all do."

Jacob wondered if that was true. In a way, he had always been a soldier for the Resistance, doing his bit for the good fight, fighting the Regime on a front that he could win. He had smuggled hundreds of amulets, and risked his life many times to do so, and while he had done it for the money, he liked to think now that he did it for a better cause. He had not realised before that everything the Resistance did, every battle they

21

fought, had given him a longer lease of life, an extra day to smuggle something in. He had often thought that he deserved thanks for all the risks he took, but he never considered that he should be giving thanks, and be giving it in good measure.

When Jacob left the engine room behind, he passed by several rooms filled to the brim with fuel. There was more room for coal than there was for crew. He wondered if, like the Lifemaker, it would eventually run out. Given Rommond's plan, however, it seemed more likely that their blood would run out first.

Jacob's next stop on his tour of the vessel was Taberah's room. He had not seen it yet, but was certain she was not bunking up with others, especially not the Copper Vixens, who accounted for the majority of the airship's female population. Soasa had been forced to bunk with the men, to avoid conflict with her old sorority. Jacob almost wished there was a fraternity for him to fall out with.

Taberah's quarters were smaller than they were on the Lifemaker, but so were everyone else's. The door was open, and he found her sitting in front of a mirror, slowly and methodically painting her nails, like a daily ritual, a little distraction from the troubles of the world. If only those troubles could so easily be painted over.

"Why do you even bother with that?" Jacob asked, barely startling her from her cosmetic duty. "They're just going to get painted with dirt."

She did not look up. "Rommond has a saying—"

"Only one?"

"—Never go to battle without loading every gun." She looked at him with her seductive eyes, accented with a thin smudge of eyeliner. Though her face was pale, it glistened like pearls. "My beauty, my femininity, is just another weapon."

"So when we met in your bedroom that time, I guess I didn't know I was being assaulted."

"You knew."

"Maybe," Jacob said with a smile, "and maybe I liked it."

Taberah closed her makeup box with a clang, and placed it neatly on the dresser before her, another ritual, another careful, controlled gesture. "They always do."

Jacob bit his lip. He wished she would not highlight the fact that she had been with so many other men. *Hell*, he thought. *I've had my fair share of women, but I'd rather forget them*. He thought especially of Cala, the most memorable one of them all, and the one he most wanted to forget.

"So are you going to lure out Rommond with your looks?" he asked.

She feigned a smile. "You'd probably have more luck with that."

"I can never get a dress that fits just right."

"Neither can I," Taberah replied, rubbing her hand across her stomach. She had recently been forced to wear maternity clothes that Doctor Mudro supplied. They were mostly dresses, and she wore them with great reluctance, fidgeting with them frequently. When she could, she wore red, which made her look like a moving flame, with just a pallid glimmer of a face within the fire.

"Maybe you can do my makeup," Jacob said. "I always thought I was a little pale."

"Too little time in the sun."

"Too much time in the shadows."

She moved on to her mouth, which she ignited with ruby lipstick. "It seems Rommond is following suit."

"You're really worried about him, aren't you?"

"Is it that obvious?" she asked.

"It's as if I read your diary."

Taberah looked away. "You wouldn't want to know what I write in there."

Jacob paused. "What do you think he'd do?" He got the image of the general hanging from a rope in his quarters, the depression finally overcoming him. Yet if he had not cracked before, if he still struggled on after Brooklyn's death, Jacob could not see him giving up now.

"I don't know any more," Taberah replied, placing the lipstick down on the dresser. Maybe Jacob had spent too long with the Resistance, but he thought it looked like a bullet.

"We're no longer on the same page," she continued. "He's got his own diary, and he keeps me out."

"Maybe that's a good thing," Jacob said. "Different perspectives."

"He doesn't want to share his with me any more. It's not like the old days. Even on the Lifemaker when I comforted him, he was reluctant. He would only share so much. There's so much I didn't know, and still don't. I feel out of the loop. God, Jacob, I didn't even know about the bomb."

Jacob glanced around instinctively, expecting others to overhear. "Maybe that's best forgotten."

"Who knows what other secrets he's keeping?" she asked. Jacob was not entirely sure if her sentiment was genuine, or if she was just trying to plant a seed of doubt in his mind, another little manipulation. If Rommond fell, would she rise to take his place?

The flicker in her eyes betrayed her. The fire that consumed her outwardly, consumed her inside as well. Jacob could not help but think: *Who knows what other secrets you're keeping too?*

Few dared knock upon the door of Rommond's quarters, and yet almost everyone aboard the airship desired to do so. Even Taberah kept her knuckles clean, and it was likely not a lack of confidence, but a certainty that she was not welcome. Rommond gave directions by periodically shoving a piece of paper under his door, guiding them towards land, and towards Blackout.

Jacob grew restless. The sense of uncertainty on the ship was growing. Nerves were frayed. It was too much for Jacob to just sit and wait, to not have answers to his many questions. He thought if he could not smuggle them out of Rommond's room, he could smuggle himself inside.

He sent Whistler on a mission, which the boy was all too eager to fulfil, to steal the plans for the airship from the Copper Vixens. Many aboard the vessel said the Matron was as good as blind, but she always seemed to spot Jacob whenever he was skulking about. Whistler seemed to have better luck.

A natural, Jacob thought. *If only I was that good when I was his age.* He almost did not want to think the next thought, but it pushed itself to the surface. *Maybe I wouldn't have had to live in a workhouse. Maybe I would've had a proper childhood.*

In time Whistler procured a schematic of the Skyshaker, which showed how to get from one part to another, through the complex system of ventilation shafts, necessary for when the vessel switched to crusader mode. The maps were bewildering, but it was less confusing than wandering those routes without them.

"You did good, kid," Jacob said. "Becoming a right little smuggler."

Whistler beamed. He had filled out his patchwork clothes a little more since his days in the Hold, but he was still thin and lanky, and stood with an awkward droop. Jacob thought that it was good to see him with his chin held high for a change.

"You're becoming a bad influence," Mudro said, appearing as if from nowhere. The smoke should have been a giveaway, but sometimes it was the shroud in which he hid.

Jacob and Whistler shrugged in unison, as if to prove the point.

"See?" the doctor said. "You should look for a different job."

"Like medicine?" Whistler asked.

"Like magic," Mudro said, before producing his own copy of the Skyshaker's schematics with a twist of his wrist.

"Impressive," Jacob said, "but I think I'll stick with smuggling."

"Rommond won't like you barging in on him," the doctor warned.

"Looks like you were thinking the same thing."

"I was, but I'm not really one for crawling about … like a spider … bad leg and all." He tapped his pipe on his left leg, which he avoided leaning on. He might have had a limp, but it did little to slow him, and nothing, it seemed, to stop him from sneaking up on people.

"What happened to it?" Jacob asked.

Whistler gave him a look, as if it was a sore topic.

"A magic trick gone wrong."

"Really?"

"No. One of Taberah's crusades. I'm lucky I have any legs at all."

"Aren't we all?"

"You think she's reckless now. You should have seen her in her younger days."

"So why did you follow?"

"I don't know," the doctor said. "She has a certain magnetism."

"You've got that right."

"Well, you should have seen her in her younger days."

"Thirty-eight's not all that old."

"In this line of work, Jacob, the life expectancy is about half that."

"I guess you've got a few years left then, Whistler," Jacob jested.

Whistler gave a reluctant smile.

"Speaking of which," the doctor said, "it's high time we got rid of those bandages. Your scars should be largely cleared up by now."

This brought a much less reluctant grin from the boy.

"I'll leave you guys to it then," Jacob said. "I'll see what scars the general has."

Mudro suddenly seized Jacob by the arm. "You might be better off letting those scab over."

Jacob clambered through the ventilation shafts, winding his way through the route Whistler had marked on the map. When he reached the end, he kicked his way through the grating into Rommond's room. He hoped the general would not think he was an intruder and greet him with a gun. *Hell*, he thought, *I hope he doesn't think it's me and use the gun anyway*.

Jacob landed on the floor with a thud, sending up a haze of dust. He coughed, partly from the debris, and partly to announce himself, though he did not really need to do the latter.

Rommond was sitting at his desk, staring over a pair of spectacles. He had a series of magnifying glasses on stands in front of him, and an assortment of springs, cogs, and other bits and bobs, most of which meant nothing to Jacob. Though the general had been locked away for days, his hair and moustache were neatly trimmed, and his uniform was as pristine as ever.

"So they sent the smuggler," Rommond said.

"Just like you to avoid using the front door."

Jacob strolled towards the door and ran his hand down a number of locks and chains. "I actually tried the front door," he said. "Sometimes that's the easiest way to smuggle something out."

"And what are you looking to smuggle out?"

"You, I think," Jacob said.

"This cargo is a little busy right now."

"I'll wait."

"You could wait outside."

Jacob saw the plaque with Brooklyn's name on it resting on Rommond's table. He tapped the metal gently, and Rommond grumbled.

"Why didn't you put it back up?"

"Every time I do, I have to take it back down again."

"Pre-empting the same eventuality?"

"It helps me to look at it."

"Inspiration?" Jacob wondered.

Rommond glanced up, with fire in his eyes. "Anger."

Jacob was silent for a time, but he roamed the room, ogling everything in sight. He heard periodic grumbles and muted coughs from Rommond.

"Am I disturbing you?" Jacob asked.

Rommond glanced up. "Always."

"Can't break the habit now."

"Is this your new addiction?" Rommond replied.

"Maybe," Jacob said with a shrug. "So, what are you making?"

"A weapon."

"I can see that."

"Then why ask?"

"What *kind* of weapon?"

"A gun that fires faster than normal."

"Why?"

"Because what the bullet strikes won't *be* normal."

"Oh?" Jacob raised an eyebrow. "I'm intrigued."

"You shouldn't be."

"What should I be then?"

"Scared."

"I thought you wanted bravery in your men."

"Bravery, yes, not naivety."

"Cure me of my naivety then. What do you plan to kill?"

Rommond raised his shoulders and lowered them slowly with a sigh.

"When we attack Blackout, they'll likely call on the Iron Guard. I want to be certain we can kill those machine men with as little as a single bullet. An armour-piercing bullet." He held up a diamond pebble, which glinted in the gaslight.

"The Iron Guard?" Jacob quizzed. "They're real? I thought they were just another fairy tale."

"The fairy tales are real, Jacob. It's humanity that is quickly becoming a myth."

"So the Regime really melded man with machine?"

"Yes," Rommond stated. "To make a monster."

"Why didn't your guys think of that?"

"We did," the general replied, "and we thought better of it. Brooklyn would never have allowed it. Some of the engineers and scientists thought we were ignoring a major opportunity to turn the tide, but

Brooklyn was adamant that it was a sin to bond metal and flesh, that in doing so we would turn the spirits of the machines against us."

"And you trusted his judgement?"

"Yes, I did, and I still do. But some didn't, and they became the root of the Armageddon Brigade, that bed of thorns that even you—inadvertently, perhaps—laid in."

"If you're talking about Cala, I didn't expect her to follow me on board."

"You have no idea what the people in the Brigade will do."

"Well, she's gone now."

"Yes, but the Brigade is not."

The general tried to delicately lodge the spring in place, but it leapt from his hands, and many of the other components sprang out with it, as if it were their rescuer.

"Blast it!" Rommond shouted. He threw the gun down on the table, where several other parts fell out. He rolled his eyes and sighed long and hard, and directly his sigh at Jacob, like a weapon of its own.

"Tricky stuff, that," Jacob said.

"I don't have what Brooklyn had."

Jacob was tempted to respond with *A gravestone?* but he thought better of it.

"He could commune with machinery like no other," Rommond continued, and he looked away wistfully. "He just knew exactly where to put every-thing, all those little springs and cogs. He said the spirits directed him, and if you had seen him work, you would have believed him. But me? No, I hear no spirit voices, and while I can fire a gun, I cannot make one. Yet I guess it is a skill that I must learn."

"Well, everyone needs a hobby."

"Did you know that I used to paint?" Rommond said.

"No."

"I used to paint a lot, before Brooklyn died." He paused, and his breathing became noticeably more shallow, as if there was not enough room inside him both for anger and breath. "Now when I see a paintbrush, all I think of is torpedoes and missiles."

"War changes us," Jacob said.

Rommond looked up. "War *ruins* us."

"You seem a little frustrated."

"Well, things aren't exactly going according to plan."

"Maybe you can't plan for everything."

"I used to be able to," Rommond said. "I could pre-empt the enemy. Now, it's not so easy."

"What has changed?"

"I don't believe in ghosts," Rommond said, "but Brooklyn's has been haunting me ever since he died."

"Maybe you need to let him go."

"Easier said than done, Jacob. I'm not sure how much of me would be left if I let him go."

"How much of you will be left if you keep clinging to the memory of him?"

Rommond sighed. "Maybe the only release is if I join him."

"I hope you're not making that gun for yourself."

Rommond smirked. "No," he said. "If I go out, I will go out fighting. If nothing else, it is what Brooklyn would have wanted. If I go down, I'll take the entire Iron Guard with me. That is, of course, if I can ever get these guns made."

"I better let you get back to work then," Jacob said. He gave a half salute, a real one this time, and turned to walk away.

"Jacob," Rommond called back.

Jacob stopped and turned.

"You didn't see anything," Rommond insisted.

"What do you mean?"

"As far as the crew know, I am unshakeable."

"But you're not," Jacob said. "None of us are."

"They don't need to know that."

"You're only human."

"To them I need to be more than that. I need to be a pillar of strength, a rock amidst the chaotic ocean, a mighty angel aloft in the sky, whose wings can never be clipped."

"That's a lot to ask of yourself."

"If no one else will take up the mantle, then it is the burden I will have to bear."

"Well, you have my support, for what it's worth."

"Maybe it is more valuable than you think," Rommond said, "more valuable than that chest of coils."

"There are a lot of rich fishes down there now."

Rommond smiled.

There was a gentle tap at the door, which betrayed the nervousness of the person on the other side. Rommond tried to suppress a sigh, but he inadvertently rolled his eyes in the direction the noise came from.

"Mice?" Jacob asked.

"As irritating as mice," Rommond stated.

"Maybe they'll go away if you give them some cheese."

"Or come back for more."

There was another rap at the door, this time a little louder, but still revealing obvious reluctance. Someone had been sent to bang on the door, perhaps to see if Rommond was all right—perhaps to see if he was still alive. Jacob thought it highly unlikely that they came to check if the same was true of him.

"Perhaps you should answer it," Jacob suggested.

"I'm busy," Rommond grumbled. He loaded another pellet, and struggled with the spring.

"They're worried about you."

"I'm worried about all of us," the general said as the bullet locked into place.

Another series of knocks followed, but no voice accompanied them. They doubtless knew they were disturbing Rommond, and wanted to limit that disturbance. Jacob wondered who it was who knocked. If it were Whistler, they likely would not have heard it at all. If it were Soasa, the door might have blown open on the first bang.

"Let them knock," Rommond said. "I have work to do."

But the knocks continued, until it seemed that at any moment the door might cave in. The rhythm was frenzied and chaotic, not like a war drum, but like a war.

"Go away!" Rommond called out. There was no response. That was undoubtedly just how Rommond liked it. Sometimes he wanted a *Yes, sir!* Other times he just wanted some peace and quiet. With Jacob there, there was little chance of that.

Then there was a sudden loud banging on the door, faster and louder than any that had come before. There was an urgency in the sound, like an alarm. Rommond appeared about to growl, but he was cut off by a frenzied voice on the other side of the door. It sounded like Boulder.

"Pirates, General! Pirates!"

Rommond stood up quickly and marched to the door. What he had spent so long locking, he unlocked in a fraction of the time. Jacob followed him out onto the main deck, which was eerily quiet, and eerily empty of people. The wind had died down, as if it too had heard the news and found itself a hiding place. The only thing worse than seeing a ghost ship in the distance was being on one.

Rommond grabbed a spyglass from the navigation tools nailed to the wall. "Where?" he asked, and Boulder pointed to the south-west. Rommond cast his angered gaze in that direction, and as he stared, he stepped forward, until he met with the fencing that stopped anyone from plummeting far below, where they might in their descent have met the pirates coming up to greet them.

Chapter Three

PIRATES OF SEA AND SKY

Far below, in the great expanse of the Last Sea, which had for the past three months served as their last haven, five galleons sailed at great speeds, their sails hoisted high, and their black flags hoisted higher. Then, just as they came close enough to where the Skyshaker cast a faint reflection in the waters, great cannons pounded, and out of them came not bullets or balls, but balloons, which hoisted the ships even higher than their pirate flags. In moments the vessels sailed out of the water and into the sky, and new cannons came into the spyglass view of the horrified crew of the Skyshaker, and these did not carry rubber and air—they carried lead and gunpowder.

"Starboard guns," Rommond called out, and he obeyed his own order by firing his revolver at one of the advancing airships. The bullet sliced through the balloon, which sent the vessel back down slowly to the sea below.

The pirate ships answered with a volley of cannon fire, all of them grazing the Skyshaker as it hurtled through the air. Rommond knew the pirates did not really want to sink it; they wanted to commandeer it—though they likely would have no problem sinking the crew, and commandeering their belongings.

"Forty degrees," Rommond said to his crew as they rolled the cannons into place. "Take out the flagship." He pointed at the Red Serpent, the largest of the galleons, the one whose black flag bore a coiling ruby snake, flicking its tongue. Rommond bit his own at the sight of it.

"Fire," he ordered. The cannons boomed in unison, but the cannonballs missed their target. Not because their aim was off, but because the flagship easily evaded the metal rain. Like a snake, it slithered from their grasp.

The cannons roared, and the engines whizzed, and the sails creaked, and the crew panted and heaved, and sighed and groaned, while the pirates shouted and jeered, until every sound tried to commandeer each other.

As the sun sank, the pirates ascended. Night was fast approaching with its own black flag to conquer day. What pallid glimmers the sun still dared to show, like the glitter of gold to tempt the thieves of sea and sky, merely illuminated the dark galleons that swiftly rose to meet the Skyshaker in the ocean of clouds.

"Take down the other ones!" Rommond barked, when it seemed the Red Serpent would simply dance like a cobra to a charmer.

By this stage the ships were almost at the same height as the Skyshaker, and now they fired grappling hooks, which clung to the sides of the vessel like the pirates' claws would soon cling to the throats of the crew.

"Get them down!" the general boomed, like

a cannon of his own. He fired at one of the ropes, which frayed, but did not sever.

Boulder rolled onto the top deck, casting a bundle of swords to the ground, and casting his hands upon his knees to stop him bowling over. He tried to pant out some words, but no one there needed direction. They knew what they had to do.

Jacob grabbed one of the swords and began hacking at the ropes tethering the pirate ships to the Skyshaker. He felled two before he heard the pellet of bullets, and felt them sailing by, like tiny pirate ships looking for the greatest treasure of all: blood. At the third rope, when Jacob raised his blade, a bullet struck it with such force that it knocked the sword from his hand. He was glad it was not his life.

It seemed as soon as ropes were cut, more appeared, like a many-headed hydra. Those snakes wound their way around the hull of the airship, clinging to the railings, clutching to the masts, and forming bridges for the other vipers who piloted the pirate ships.

The invasion began in an instant, and though guns were fired, and the Copper Vixens flooded the deck, each with duel pistols, and though the air filled with smoke and steam, and the ground filled with gunpowder and bullet casings, the pirates swung into place, dodging the many missiles aimed at them, or clinging to falling ropes, only to launch themselves across the cloudy ravine on yet another one.

Then the bullets were mostly spent, and though many on either side fell, many were left, and all they had were swords. The fight began anew, and the pirates threw themselves forward in a frenzy, hissing like serpents, eyeing everyone in sight with a mad lust, waving their cleavers and curved swords as if the very sky were attacking them.

Rommond did not baulk at this display, but simply walked into the fray, slicing with the sword in his right hand, and firing with the revolver in his left. He was conservative with his shots, keeping them for when a pirate was about to land a killing blow on one of his crew, or when he could fire a ricochet shot that struck several of the pirates at once, and reinforced one of his many nicknames. He waded through the onslaught, which seemed never-ending, and Jacob found himself back to back with the general, swinging his own sword, and wishing he had a gun instead.

Then the Skyshaker rocked, and many stumbled, and they cast their eyes to the starboard side, where the pirate flagship had docked. Latches in the shape of cobra heads locked into place, clutching the railing of the airship in their metal fangs.

The battle ceased for a moment, with the pirates stepping back, but still barking and booing, hissing and hooting. The Copper Vixens manned the other side, holding each other back, issuing their own insults, bashing their breasts and brandishing their blades.

Then the pirates pushed a plank across from their flagship to the Skyshaker, and across it stepped the leader of their little armada, in which they were certain they were about to add another ship.

Chapter Four

THE SNAKE

The pirate leader was a short and slender man with a tanned complexion and golden-brown locks, close enough to Jacob in age, though nowhere near as rough or rugged. He was clean-shaven, and he had a glistening smile, accented by several gold teeth. His dazzling blue eyes matched the rich blues of his long coat and tricorne hat, which had a number of feathers in it from now extinct birds. His belt was laden with many swords and daggers. Jacob thought that there was something very familiar about him.

The corsair captain approached slowly, while his crew stayed back. He did not so much as move, but dance. All his gestures were animated. All his words were spoken with excitement, like a child who talks about his toys. But he was the kind of child who took the toys of others, and a new one had entered his sight.

Rommond glared at him. "The Snake," he hissed.

The pirate grinned. "The Hawk," he replied, and he flapped his hands. "I see your eyes are as good as ever." Then he swivelled on the spot, more elegantly than any pirate had ever moved in the history of hijacking, and he bowed before the other onlookers, as if he expected their applause. "Samadan El Abra. I would say, 'at your service', but I think maybe you are more at mine."

"You won't get this ship," Rommond stated. "I'd rather let it burn."

"Such a waste!" El Abra declared, like he declared everything, sending his arms to the sky, eliciting a gasp from the Copper Vixens, as if he was throwing a grenade. "Why, you're lucky you use helium and not hydrogen in this beauty, or it might already be burning."

"You're lucky that you still use oxygen," Rommond replied. "We can change that easily enough."

"Come now, let us settle this with honour."

Rommond scoffed. "There's nothing honourable in piracy."

"Some might say there's nothing honourable in war, yet you still wage it."

"When fighting demons, everything we do is honourable."

"Perhaps, but what about before the Harvest? You fought in plenty of other wars back then."

"And you plundered plenty of ships, more than your fair due."

"I am due what I can take," El Abra said. He held his arms up and turned around, taking in the view. "And this, Rommond, is ripe for the taking. Why, I've never seen anything like it. What do you call it?"

"The Skyshaker," Rommond replied, and his pride was like another medal, pinned visibly to his immaculate uniform.

"Oooh," the pirate said. "Makes me shiver. I

haven't heard a name like that in quite some time. Not since the good old days." He showed his golden teeth once more.

"When we played cat and mouse," the general said.

"You never did catch me then, did you? Gold-wall's golden boy, with more medals than space on your coat to pin them. But you never got the medal for getting me."

"Maybe I'll earn it now," Rommond said.

"Who from, I wonder?" the pirate asked. "If you couldn't do it with that battleship you had—what did you call it? Wavewalker? You always were one for fancy names—then I think your luck is up."

Rommond could barely hide his contempt behind his walrus moustache. If he could have grown tusks to bare at the pirate, he would have bore them now.

"Whatever did happen to that ship?" El Abra teased.

Rommond glared at him. "I might have lost the ship," he said, "but I see the mouse has lost none of its smugness."

El Abra's smile only widened. "Now I'm the cat."

Taberah leapt at him from out of nowhere, like a rabid lynx, but what others did not see, he saw, and he simply sidestepped out of the way.

"Mademoiselle!" El Abra cried, while parrying Taberah's frenzied strikes and backing away. "Do you not remember? I do not fight women!"

"That's fine by me," Taberah said, and lunged at him again. "Just so long as you don't mind dying at a woman's hands."

"It would be a pleasure," El Abra said, simultaneously raising an eyebrow and the side of his mouth. "Especially one as beautiful and elegant as you, even when with child." He eyed Rommond, as if he assumed that he was the father. "But alas! I cannot fight you, unless it were a fight with lips. Till then, I must ask you to leave this to the owner of this fair vessel, which might be a little fairer with a different owner."

Yet Taberah would not back down. She sliced and struck, and El Abra blocked and backed away once more. He looked to Rommond with a hint of discontentment.

"You allow this?" he asked. "Tell her to stop before she gets hurt. Unless, of course, there's not a hint of honour in you, General, and you have women fight your battles."

"My battles, no," Rommond said. "They fight their own."

El Abra waved his sword before Rommond as a challenge. "Perhaps you will dare to fight yours then? Unless all you do is rely on feisty women, and your trademark trick shots, *Ricochet Rommond*."

Taberah prepared to attack again, but Rommond held up his hand. "Wait," he said. "Leave this to me." In most cases she would not have listened, but he looked her straight in the eyes, and hoped she understood: *You got Domas. El Abra is mine.*

Rommond stepped into the ring, a literal ring of pirates and Copper Vixens, who looked as though they were about to fight amongst themselves at any moment. Yet they waited, holding back their hate, such was the respect they had for their leaders.

The general waved his pistol in the air, before discarding it to the floor. He unleashed his sword, a mostly ceremonial weapon, which had seen far more than ceremony in the trenches of the war's early years.

"Who shall strike first?" El Abra said. "I know! The one who lost last time."

This angered Rommond more than Jacob thought it should, and the general swung at the pirate, who parried and span out of the way, leading Rommond after him in a trail of misdirection that might have impressed Mudro, were the doctor not watching the fight with a frown.

Taberah stood beside Jacob, arms folded in defiance. At times she twitched and fidgeted, and it was clear that she was fighting her instinct to join the fray. Jacob placed his hand on her shoulder, but she shrugged it off, as if it were El Abra's.

The pirate flitted delicately across the deck, barely making a sound, bar the whirring and purring of his sword. Each time he passed close enough to Taberah, he purred a line of his own: "Radiant!" he cried. "Rousing!" he simpered. "Regal!" he bellowed like her rightful king. Then he started on the words that began with 's,' whispering "Sensual" in a way that every woman present, and quite a few men, heard it in their hearts.

"I've got to hand it to him," Jacob said with a smirk. "He's doing wonders on me."

Taberah elbowed him. To her, a compliment from an enemy was an insult. To Jacob, who had hard so few compliments in his life, it did not matter where they came from.

As El Abra talked and taunted, and as he traipsed about the deck like a joyful child, Jacob could not help but be reminded of someone he once knew. It had been so long, and the name was different, but the mannerisms were the same. Age changed many things, but others it left untouched, or merely accentuated. El Abra's balletic movements were one of these.

This dance made things worse for Rommond, who struggled to keep up. As elegantly as El Abra swung, Rommond cleaved, using strength when he found he could not match the pirate's speed. The general's steps were clumsy, more of a jittering jive to El Abra's effortless waltz.

The crowd around began to cheer or jeer, depending on which side they were on. It was as if the very fate of the ship really did lie in this outcome, as if Rommond would give it up willingly if he lost, or El Abra would retreat if the general won. Whistler jumped up and down behind the Copper Vixens, trying to get a better view, and joining in the zealous chants of Rommond's name.

"Enough!" Rommond called out, stopping in his tracks like a halting landship. He unleashed a grenade from his belt, which caught El Abra off-guard, knocking him from his feet.

"You didn't dodge that," the general said.

The pirate humphed. "Dirty tricks," he groaned.

"No," Rommond said. "This is just my kind of dance."

El Abra stood up and dusted himself off. "So, you don't fancy your chances toe to toe."

"You don't fancy yours, bomb to limb."

They circled each other, mocking and jeering, which elicited *oohs* and *aahs* from the crowd, as if their blades had struck anew. It was as much a battle of wits and words as it was of mitts and swords. It seemed as if they were building up for another round, but the audience was so enthralled, and cheered so loudly, that this might as well have been round two.

As Jacob watched, he continued to rack his brain, trying to place the figure among the many figures of his past. In time the memory surfaced from the prison of his mind.

"I know him," Jacob said, though his recollection of him was quite different to what he had become. "He was another workhouse boy, forced to pay his parents' debts. I guess that doesn't leave much options for a career path: smuggling or piracy."

"Can you reason with him?" Taberah asked.

"I'm not sure. We kind of had a … friendly rivalry."

"So long as it was friendly," Mudro said.

"Well, as much of a friendship anyone could form in the workhouses. I got out before him. Part of me felt guilty. I never liked to take the route past there, as it would remind me that he was still inside, toiling away, like those people in the Hope factory. I never saw him after that."

"So how do you know it's him?"

"You don't forget Samuel," Jacob replied. "That

was his name back then. He's quite a character."

And that he was.

Rommond and El Abra looked about to go to blows again, when Jacob interrupted.

"Samuel," Jacob said, visibly startling El Abra. If Rommond had not been so tired from the previous fight, he might have taken advantage of the pirate's lapse.

"Do I know you?" the Snake asked.

"I guess I'm not as memorable as *you* are," Jacob said.

El Abra beamed at this comment, and gave a slight curtsy, all the while casting his eyes at each and every woman in sight.

"Do you remember Olbaron's seven rules?" Jacob enquired. Few could forget those workhouse rules, or Olbaron's cruel punishments if they were broken. For many, the memories were branded into their skin.

"Jacob?" El Abra asked, holding his sword up to keep Rommond at bay. He blinked a few times to take in the sight of his old friend.

"Yes. It's been some time."

"So it has. And not a time I like to be reminded of. I'm surprised you do."

"We had a difficult life back then. Maybe we can make it less difficult now."

"I intend to," El Abra said. "I've been making up for those days for quite some time."

"Rob from the Treasury then."

"Oh, I have, when they take to the air. Land just doesn't cut it for me."

"Not a land thief?"

"Not a land anything. I haven't set foot on that scorched earth in years. Why walk when you can swim or fly?"

"A snake afraid of sand," Rommond mused.

"A hawk who has only recently learned how to fly," El Abra countered.

"With demons taking over," Jacob said, "you'd imagine we'd be more keen to be human."

"There's something powerful about animals," El Abra said. "Something primal. It's no wonder the tribes go mad for them. You should pick one."

"I already have one," Jacob replied. "Well, kind of. A spider."

El Abra laughed heartily. "Maybe you should try again."

Jacob forced a chuckle. "So, given everything we suffered together, maybe you can let us go?"

El Abra did not need to force his own. "I wouldn't make a very good pirate then, would I?"

"You'd make a good friend."

Something changed in El Abra's eyes, like a shadow of a memory, but it passed just as quickly. "That was a friendship of convenience, Jacob."

"Not to me."

"Then how come when you got out, I never saw you again?"

"I don't know," Jacob said. "Life happened."

"Life happened to me as well, Jacob. It brought me to where I am right now."

"So, you won't let us go?"

"Jacob, I will do this one favour for you: you can take a raft, or a balloon, or whatever it is that

Rommond has tucked away up the Skyshaker's sleeves, and you can escape here alive. Or better yet, why not come and work for me?"

"I worked *with* you long enough in my childhood."

"Working *for* me is a lot more fun," the pirate said. "You get to play with the toys."

The memories were barbed; the wire connected from Jacob's brain to his heart. It could not be cut—the barbs dug in too deep. He tried to suppress them, tried to bury them below deck, out of view, out of reach. But even there he could see his little hands at work, carving little wooden horses for other children's games.

"I've already got a job," Jacob said, gulping down the words, choking on the memories.

"Fighting for the Resistance? It doesn't seem your style."

Jacob could not say the same about El Abra. Piracy was just his style.

"Fighting the good fight," Jacob said.

"I'm living the good life," El Abra said, "for once."

"That's the life I thought I wanted too. It doesn't look so glamorous any more."

Rommond coughed loudly. "If this childhood friendship means nothing today, then perhaps we can get back to our adult rivalries. If you try to take this ship, Snake, then I'll make sure we all go up in flames. Then we can share reminiscences forever in the depths of Hell."

El Abra laughed. "Always one to bluff."

"Try me," the general said, and it seemed that he might ignite a bomb at any moment. The battle looked as though it was about to begin anew, and more fiercely than ever, with pirate and Vixen reaching for their swords and guns.

Suddenly Taberah cried out and keeled over, clutching her stomach. Jacob tried to support her, and all eyes, even those of Rommond and El Abra, looked towards her.

"A temporary truce," El Abra declared, putting his swords away.

Rommond nodded and ran over to Taberah. "What's wrong?" he asked.

"I don't know," she said. "The baby."

"You can't be giving birth now!" Jacob cried. "It's too soon."

Chapter Five

FALSE FLAG

Taberah groaned, and Mudro urged her to breathe deeply, which only resulted in louder moans. She struck out at anyone around, especially El Abra, who crouched down with many of the others, offering his aid, putting aside his prior differences, which she most certainly could not put aside.

"It's coming now," she screamed, and the worry leapt from face to face, until the entire crowd was concerned about the fate of the baby. "She's a Pure," they whispered to one another, knowing how important that little life in her was. They were the pirates of today, but it might be the pirate of tomorrow.

"Listen to me," Mudro told her, clutching her hand, while she squeezed his tight. "You've got to calm down and slow your breath. We want this to pass."

"How far is she?" El Abra asked.

"Three and a half months," Rommond said reluctantly.

El Abra said nothing, but his face said enough: it was much too soon, much too early. That little pirate might only get to pilfer enough breath for today.

Whistler paced up and down the deck behind the

Copper Vixens, despite being told to go to the lower levels. His bandages had been removed, and Mudro had worked his magic on the boy's scars, but to witness the early birth—and early death—of his little brother or sister might leave new ones that magic could not remove.

Taberah grabbed Jacob's hand. "I left a charm below deck," she said with a shudder. "A birth charm that Brooklyn gave me. Bring me it, please." She looked deep into his eyes, communicating something, but he was not entirely sure what she meant.

"I'll get it," El Abra volunteered.

"No," she said. "He's the father."

El Abra nodded to his crew, who blocked the way into or out of the lower levels, where the Resistance might find more weaponry, or more reinforcements. They, rather reluctantly, let Jacob slip through, but disarmed him in the process, as if he might somehow work some mischief with his sword. He only needed his bare hands for that.

Jacob hurried down to Taberah's quarters, but he could not find the charm. There was little furniture or possessions to root through, but in his search his eyes found the words on an opened page of her diary, and he could not help but read them: *The pains are worse today. I'm hoping they will pass. I dare not tell anyone my fear.* He was tempted to read more, but he thought it best not to, and he could not delay, lest indeed her fear did come to pass.

At first he did not realise, but he found that he was also looking for something else. Part of him would have even traded the birth charm for it, if there was anyone there to trade with. Taberah had her own cravings, which found her in Karlsif's kitchen late at night, but the one Jacob felt right then was stronger than anything, almost stronger than him. He was looking for Hope.

It was a great struggle just to suppress that desire, that want, that need. It almost felt like a different person, a hungry person, a starving demon. As he tried to bury it, it tried to bury him. His muscles ached, as if he were fighting an invisible enemy. It was strong, but his feelings for Taberah and their child was stronger. He locked away that lust for Hope, and focused on his mission, his duty, that little thing that Taberah wanted for the little thing inside her.

He began to frantically run about below deck, asking the few crew he found there where he could find Taberah's birth charm, which was answered only by confused glances. He did not know what to do. He ran his fingers through his hair, as if he could find the answer there. Then it dawned on him: the one thing that would definitely help the birth was to get El Abra off the ship, by any means necessary. He needed a gun, a big gun, and he thought it would work like a charm.

Above deck, the two factions continued their uneasy truce, focusing their attention on Taberah, who periodically moaned and shouted, and frequently cursed at the pirates, as if all of them had done this to her. Rommond joined Whistler in his restless pacing, while Mudro continued his attempts to slow or stop the birth process.

"I don't understand," the doctor said after his latest investigation. "If the contractions are that bad, you should be having it now. I don't see the baby. It's not ready yet."

Taberah looked at Mudro with fire in her eyes, as if he had let out the game.

"If this baby isn't coming," El Abra said, "then I think we better finish what we started."

"Go back to your own vessel then," Rommond replied.

"Sorry Rommond," El Abra said. "It's business. Pure business." He unsheathed his sword again, and the glint of the blade made it look like it was personal.

Then the cabin exploded in splinters, and out rolled the Hopebreaker like a pet summoned to its master's plea. Rommond's subtle smile was masked behind his not so subtle moustache.

The gun barrel turned and lowered to where El Abra stood in shock.

"You and your toys," the pirate said. "I kind of wanted a go of that."

"I'll let you try the gun," Rommond replied, just a split second before the turret fired, knocking El Abra back and off the side of the ship. The turret turned to the other pirates, who did not take long diving over the edge of their own accord, landing on the deck of one of the galleons below, where, if El Abra was lucky, his remains had fallen. The fangs of the Red Serpent withdrew, and the ship headed back down to the sea below, out of range of the Hopebreaker's missiles.

Rommond breathed a sigh of relief, and looked with bemusement at his favourite landship, which was an imposing sight on the open deck. For a moment he almost thought that Brooklyn had designed it too well, that it had suddenly come to life, and would fire at the enemies of its master without a driver. He patted the chassis, as he might pet a dog. Though he did not know how it came to his call, he knew one thing for sure: the Hopebreaker had bark, and it had bite.

Then the hatch opened and out popped Jacob, who grinned at the general, like anyone might have grinned if they had the opportunity to drive and fire that imperial vehicle.

"Thank you," Rommond said, tipping his cap.

Jacob gave a mock salute.

"Just don't touch the Hopebreaker again," the general said.

"I'll save you next time with your own pistol," Jacob jeered.

"I don't think there will be a next time with him." Rommond glanced overboard to where the pirates were swiftly retreating.

Jacob jumped down and ran to Taberah, who was standing and dusting herself off. "I couldn't find the charm," he called to her. "Are you all right? Did Mudro manage to stop it?"

"I wasn't really giving birth," she replied.

Jacob shook his head, confused. "You were faking it?"

"Of course," she said. "I know El Abra's weaknesses. So-called honour is one of them. It was a good distraction."

"But you seemed like you were really in pain."

"It's only been three and a half months. I'm not ready to have this baby yet."

"Oh."

"Don't look so disappointed."

"Yeah, I suppose it's better that it stays in the oven. Don't want it undercooked."

"I don't want it overcooked either," Taberah replied.

She grabbed his shoulder suddenly and closed her eyes tight, as if a sharp pain had seized her. Her breathing was heavy, and her face was flushed.

"Are you all right?" Jacob asked.

"Yes, just a little tense. Can you walk me to my quarters?"

As Jacob did so, supporting her as she walked slowly, watching her as she cringed with each and every step, something told him that the pains she felt, the pains she said she feigned, were very real.

Chapter Six

COLD TURKEY

"Well, that was exciting," Whistler said, when Jacob emerged above deck again. The boy chewed his nails, only stopping to bite his lip.

Jacob widened his eyes. "Nerve-wrecking, more like."

"Yeah."

There was an awkward silence.

"So, that guy, that pirate," Whistler said, "was he your friend?"

"Yeah, a long time ago. Seems like a different age."

"You don't shoot all your friends, do you?"

Jacob chuckled. "Only the good ones."

He might have laughed outwardly, but he was not amused inside. What guilt he felt that he had left El Abra in the workhouse when they were young, that he had abandoned him when he got out, and never tried to find him later, was only magnified by the barrel of the Hopebreaker's gun. He might have killed the pirate, but he could not kill his shame.

"Why didn't he help?" Whistler asked.

"What do you mean?"

"Isn't that what friends are supposed to do? He could have helped us take back Blackout."

Jacob sighed. "In an ideal world, sure, but it's not as simple as that, kid. We kind of parted ways, took different paths. I guess I wasn't a good enough friend to him."

"You are to me," Whistler said.

Jacob smiled. He might have ruffled the boy's hair, were it not already well ruffled beneath his faded hat. "So, were you ready for a little brother or sister?"

Whistler scrunched his mouth. "I'm not sure. I suppose so." He paused and took off his peaked beret, which he gripped tightly with both hands, letting his red-brown curls tumble freely. "Were you ready for a little son or daughter?"

Jacob shrugged. He had no hat to take off, and nothing to hold. "You know, I'm not sure either. It would have been funny if it was born today though."

"Why's that?"

"It's my birthday."

"Oh," Whistler said. "Well ... happy birthday."

"Thanks, though I've had happier."

"How old are you now? A hundred?"

"Cheeky. Thirty-six. What a hell of a birthday."

"Better than mine," Whistler said, looking to his well-worn shoes, as if they had been a birthday gift.

Jacob raised an eyebrow. "Why? What happened then?"

"I spent it in the Hold."

"Hell," Jacob said. "I'm sorry. So you turned fourteen in that cell?"

"Yes. Well, I think so. I lost track of the days. I suppose with the constant darkness, it all seemed like one long night. All I know is I went in when I was thirteen, and I came out fourteen. Or so Doctor Mudro says. He's good with calendars."

"And here I am complaining about a little sweat and stress."

"You can complain. I don't mind."

Jacob laughed. "You're a cool kid, Whistler, you know that?"

Whistler smiled and shrugged.

"I'm serious. You've been through more than most, and still you're as strong as ever."

The boy looked up. "I never really thought of myself as strong."

"Well, you are," Jacob stated, "in the ways that count the most. Anyone can build muscle. You can't build what you've got. You're born with it."

Whistler sunk his head again. "Maybe it's the demon in me."

"No, kid, it's not. It's the human in you. Hell, you're more human than the rest of us."

As night fell, Jacob sought out Mudro and told him of his Hope hunger, which had steadily increased throughout the day. The shakes returned with a frenzy, and his body felt on fire. He had been able to momentarily bury that deep yearning, but it was still there, and still alive.

"That's good," the doctor said, when Jacob described his symptoms. "It means the Greenshield is wearing off, and you're relying on your own body now to fight the Hope."

Jacob wiped his brow on his sleeve. "How's that good?"

"It's the end of the process, Jacob. If you can ride this out, you'll have essentially conquered the drug."

"And if I can't?"

"It conquers you."

"Hell, I wish she'd never forced that stuff down my throat."

Mudro handed him a handkerchief. "She's not forcing you now."

"But I've had the taste. It's better not to have the taste."

Mudro exhaled smoke from his pipe slowly. "You're right there."

"So there's nothing you can do?"

"I can give you my quarters for the night."

"I'm not really that way inclined," Jacob said.

Mudro laughed. "A private room to let the poison out. Trust me … you won't want the entire crew witnessing you falling apart. And the crew won't want to be picking up the pieces."

Jacob sighed. "I bet. How did you get your own quarters anyway? I'm stuck bunking it with Rommond's finest."

"Magic," the doctor said. "Anyway, I needed space for my medical supplies."

"There better not be any Hope there."

"I'll remove anything dangerous."

With the remnants of Hope still coursing through Jacob's veins, changing him, making it difficult for him to retain control, he could not help but think: *Maybe you'll need to remove me.*

* * *

Jacob set up for the night in Mudro's quarters, and the doctor cleared out many chests of medicines, most especially his remaining supply of Greenshield, which would only delay the process, and lead to all kinds of complications and new addictions. Mudro laid out several damp towels for Jacob, and several empty buckets, and Jacob prepared for a difficult night.

When Mudro left, and Jacob prepared to lock the door, he found Whistler outside, with bright eyes to match Jacob's dark and heavy ones.

"I overheard," he said.

"You mean you eavesdropped."

Whistler cocked his head. "I didn't have the proper apparatus."

"Pity," Jacob said. "I could have done with a drink. So, what did you hear?"

"Pretty much everything."

"Well, I won't lie. I'm having a difficult time right now."

"Maybe I can help."

"You can go," Jacob said. "This is probably not going to be a pretty sight."

"No," Whistler said. "I'm going to stay. If it were me, I think I'd want the company. I think … maybe it's easier if you've got a friend."

Jacob smiled as much as the drug would allow. He tried to hold back a tear. Though the drug made him feel like he needed something else, like he needed only it, Whistler's presence made him feel like he only needed someone else to be there, anyone to stop him feeling alone.

"Consider it a birthday gift," Whistler said.

That night was full of evils, where Jacob tossed and turned, and saw phantom figures from his past, and heard spectral voices from his memories. His mind raced, and his body ached. Sweat poured from him like a waterfall, as if the very moisture could no longer stand the husk of his body. Almost every hour he had to get up to vomit, and between each of these heavings he shouted all manner of things to the four walls of the room. Whistler sat with him throughout all of this, even when Jacob urged him to leave, and at times Jacob was ashamed that the boy witnessed this weakness of his, and at other times he was glad that he was there.

He thought of all the junkies in Blackout, and all the Hope-crazed maniacs that wandered from town to town, and he no longer felt above them, looking down. He thought of Cala and all her different highs, and all her efforts to seek the next one. He remembered her looking into the eyeboxes, and offering him the "sight," and he remembered that he refused. Now he realised that maybe instead of chasing highs, she was running from the lows. She had reached the bottom of the ocean, but she had struck the bottom of life long before that. Jacob hoped he would not one day join her there.

Chapter Seven

SPENDTHRIFT

When Jacob awoke the next morning, he found that Whistler was still there, dozing awkwardly on a chair. It was well into the afternoon, and well past Jacob's normal rising hour, but getting the last of the Hope out of him, without the counteracting benefit of Greenshield, had sapped so much of his energy, and had kept him—the both of them even—up all night.

Jacob crawled out of bed, keeping one of the damp cloths to his forehead, which pounded relentlessly. He emptied another bucket and tried to tidy up the room, without waking Whistler. He could not imagine Mudro would want to sleep there again.

He left Whistler snoring gently, and wandered about below deck. There were only two levels down there, one floor for the crew, and the other for the vehicles. It was lucky that the vessel sailed the skies mostly in cruising mode, or it might have felt even more claustrophobic than the Lifemaker.

During his roaming, Jacob encountered Soasa, who was spooning gunpowder into metal balls, and piling them up in a precarious pyramid. It seemed she was not in the least bit frightened that they might tumble and explode. Jacob stood as far away from them as possible.

"Hey Soasa," he said. "Funny bumping into you here."

Soasa scoffed. "It's not like there's much place to go. This place is so cramped."

"Cosy," Jacob said with a smile.

She glanced at him. "Sheesh, you look terrible."

"Rough night."

"Rougher than normal, you mean."

"Yeah."

"Well," she said, "what do you want?"

"A favour."

"You should try someone else."

"I don't exactly have many friends on this thing."

"Well, I don't have many either."

"I heard you're pals with the pilot."

"Cantro? We're friends since we were kids. Rommond recruited him to the Resistance early on. When Taberah made a bid for the leadership, I offered him a place in the Order."

"And he said no?"

"Well, he's flying this ship, isn't he?"

"I guess Rommond rewards loyalty."

Soasa cocked her head. "Dynamite is loyal to the one who lights the fuse."

"Well, in this situation, Cantro's my dynamite, and you're my fuse."

"I'm not interested," Soasa said as she turned back to the bombs she was preparing.

"Hear me out, Soasa, please."

Soasa sighed and placed down the gunpowder.

"Hurry then."

"I need you to convince Cantro to let Whistler fly this thing, even just for a few minutes."

"Are you mad? He wouldn't allow it."

"For you he might."

"He didn't get to be pilot by trusting airships to the hands of children."

"He can watch him, step in if things get out of hand. The kid just needs to feel like he's in control, that he can fly this thing."

Soasa shook her head. "It's not gonna happen."

"Come on, Soasa," Jacob pleaded. "It's not for me."

Soasa scoffed. "Even good deeds we do for others, we do for ourselves."

"I'm not that cynical."

"You should be. This world doesn't teach anything else."

"*We* do."

"Why do you care about him?" Soasa asked.

"I don't know. Why *don't* you care about him?"

"I care. Just … well, I guess I'm just not the mothery type."

"You don't have to be. Just be the type that does a favour for a friend."

"Friends, are we?" she replied.

Jacob smiled, and Soasa sighed.

"I'll help you," she said, "for a price."

"You know that I lost my fortune, right?"

"All of it?" she asked, as if she knew he could not be that bad a gambler.

"The crate was on the Lifemaker when it went down."

Soasa's eyes widened. "And you didn't try to save it?"

"I was … preoccupied."

"With what? It must have been quite something for you to give up that much money."

"It was. You could say I was a bit absent-minded."

"So you're penniless now?"

"It's been a long time since we used pennies, Soasa. But yeah. Well, almost. I have five coils left. They were in my pocket when we fled the Lifemaker."

"Okay then," Soasa said. "I'll do it for five."

Jacob sighed, and took out the coils. A little family of coils. "This is all I have left."

"It's less than I should be charging."

"I'll have nothing then."

"You'll have a new-found cynicism."

Jacob humphed. He held the coils up, rolled one between his fingers, and flicked another into the air. The clink was still reassuring, but the sound seemed dull. Even the colour appeared sapped of its vibrancy. It was as if for the first time, he could really see that these were made of iron, not gold.

He handed the remnants of his fortune over to Soasa. "I guess I'm really penniless now."

"Thank Rommond he doesn't charge you rent."

"Why do you want the coils anyway?" Jacob asked. "Doesn't the Resistance provide everything you need?"

"What, like explosives?"

"That … and food."

"Yeah, I get my rations like all the rest."

"So what do you need the coils for?"

Soasa looked away, and it seemed that she was thinking of far-off places. "I'm not entirely sure this war is for me."

"I don't think it's for anyone."

"Yeah, but … I wasn't really in it for 'the cause.'"

"Kindred spirits," Jacob said. "What were you here for?"

Soasa rubbed her hands through her short hair, dotting it with gunpowder. "The people."

"All of them?" Jacob asked. "Or someone in particular?"

"Certainly not you, that's for sure."

"What? Am I not your type?"

Soasa smiled. "Not exactly."

"So is this your retirement fund?"

Soasa cast her gaze towards the east, where the Iron Empire's grip was as strong as ever. "I don't really think we're going to win this thing."

"We mightn't if we lose our Dynamite Lady."

Soasa humphed. "I think you'll manage just fine."

"From you that almost sounds like a compliment."

"Manage, not win. I think the deck is stacked against us."

"I've won before on a bad hand."

"By bluffing?"

"A bit of that, and a bit of daring. Sometimes all the players get a bad hand. You just have to be determined enough to see the game through."

"Well, I don't share your optimism. For me, I just …" but she paused and sighed again. She cast her gaze to the west, where the Iron Empire's grip was weakest, and yet still could be felt. "I want to get away, settle down somewhere."

"Somehow I can't imagine that life for you."

"I can," she said wistfully. "I've imagined it for a long time."

"And what would you do?"

"I want a house, a garden, a little patch of land to call my own. Somewhere I can grow things."

"I'm not sure you can grow dynamite."

Soasa chortled. "There's more to me than dynamite, you know."

"So it seems. You just never struck me as the settled type."

"Well, what I dream, and what I do in reality, they're quite far apart."

"So where would you go? There's not exactly lots of grassland left in Altadas."

"Probably somewhere up near Copperfort, or further north."

"So you'd just sit around all day growing vegetables?"

"Something like that."

"Well, I find it hard to visualise," Jacob said, and he squinted his eyes, as if that might make it easier. "I'm trying to imagine what kind of life that would be for Taberah. If we win this war, what will she end up doing? I can't quite see her tending the hearth."

Soasa looked away. "No," she said bitterly. "No, I can't either."

"So, would you live alone?"

"Probably."

"No family?"

She rolled her eyes at him. "It's not exactly like

that's possible for me. I'm not a Pure."

"You could still have a couple of little demon rascals running around the place."

Soasa was clearly less amused than Jacob was by this.

"But if you could," Jacob continued, "would you have a family?"

Soasa sighed. "I guess I'd like that."

"So maybe you're more the mothery type than you think."

"Maybe," Soasa said. She held up the five coils Jacob had given her. "I'll look after these, at least. And I make no promises about Cantro. If he agrees, he agrees. Otherwise, no refunds."

Jacob nodded. He thought that if she got Cantro to agree, the look on Whistler's face would be all the payment he would need.

Chapter Eight

KING OF THE CLOUDS

"Where are we going?" Whistler asked. "It's a surprise."

"I'm not sure I like surprises."

"You'll like this one."

Jacob nudged the boy forward, and held his hands over his eyes. They waddled across the top deck, and some of the crew giggled as they passed.

"Are they laughing at us?" Whistler asked.

"I think they're laughing at me."

"You're not, like, going to throw me off the ship, are you?"

Jacob chuckled. "No, of course not."

"Well, that would be a surprise."

"Yeah, I suppose it would. But trust me, kid, you'll like this one. Now, we're coming to some steps. Step up. And again. And once more."

They reached the top of the pilot's platform, where Cantro, a broad figure with a grim face and a huge, angular jaw, stood. He steered the ship with a giant wheel and a series of levers, which connected with a matrix of cogs, pulleys, and pistons. Two large chimney stacks stood on either side of the wheel, one spewing smoke, the other spewing steam, though they spewed nothing at all when the vessel switched to crusader mode.

"I smell smoke," Whistler said. "Is something burning?"

Jacob removed his hands from Whistler's eyes, and Whistler looked about. He had not been allowed this close to the platform before, let alone walk upon it. He smiled broadly.

"I get to meet the captain?" Whistler asked, looking to Jacob.

"You get to *be* the captain," Jacob replied.

Whistler was visibly shocked. His smile faded, but not because he was not happy. He clearly did not know how to feel. His eyes welled up, and he bit his lip to stop it from quivering.

Jacob ushered him closer to the wheel, and it seemed that Cantro was making every effort to restrain himself at the sight of anyone else bar Rommond or Taberah touching the controls.

"Well, go on then," Jacob said, and he placed Whistler's hands upon the wheel.

The boy stood there for a moment, staring at the wheel, not moving his hands, not turning it, in some ways using it for support. He looked at Jacob.

"I don't know what to do."

Cantro stepped in to show him the ropes, and Jacob stepped back to let Whistler enjoy his tutorial. Whistler looked at him with a hidden joy awoken in his eyes. "Thank you," he whispered.

"Consider it a late birthday gift," Jacob replied with a smile.

He caught Whistler's cap when it blew off in a

ferocious gust of wind. "Woah!" he said. "You'll need that ... captain." He placed it back on Whistler's head.

And so Cantro guided Whistler's hands, tilting the wheel, pulling the levers, switching on the pistons. He showed him how to adjust the sail, how to fire up the engines, how to change speeds. From the most basic to the most complex, Cantro taught the boy how to fly the airship, and Whistler picked up everything with ease, much to the amazement of all onlookers.

In time Whistler felt confident enough with the controls, and Cantro felt confident enough to let him fly unaided, and so the boy became the pilot of the hour, guiding the Skyshaker through the clouds, following the coordinates that Rommond had laid out.

And as he flew, Whistler shouted to the sky. "Woo!" he cried, as if he had just grown his very own wings.

Jacob laughed and cheered. From the corner of his eye he saw Taberah standing at the bottom of the steps, her arms folded, and instead of a scowl on her face, there was a smile. Jacob looked at her, and she at him, and they both looked to Whistler, yelling gleefully to the wind, and they could not help but feel some of that same glee.

The Skyshaker glided through the clouds with as much ease as if Cantro himself was steering it. He might have stopped someone else much sooner, but Whistler was clearly a natural, and few could watch him fly the vessel and want to stop him.

The smile on the boy's face was like none he had

ever given before. It was certainly the broadest since he found out that Domas was his father, and perhaps the happiest since he was born. He turned to Jacob with that smile, with that glint in his eyes, the wind in his hair, and the sun gleaming like a halo around him, like a glistening crown for a new king of the clouds.

Chapter Nine

TARGET ACQUIRED

When everyone heard the latches on Rommond's door opening, the celebration ended, and the screeching bolts reminded them that the war was still raging, and that one of its greatest battles was ahead of them. Cantro took the wheel once more, and the crew returned swiftly to their duties.

"It's time," Rommond said. "I've drawn up our targets."

Taberah glared at him. She had been left out of the meeting.

Rommond marched to the centre of the gondola, and his lieutenants hurriedly hauled several barrels and planks of wood over to assemble a makeshift table. He placed a large map down just as the last wooden panel was slotted into place.

"Here," he said, stabbing the map with his index finger, "is our first port of call."

"Is that an armoury?" Taberah asked.

"Yes, Tabs, and the largest one in Blackout. That needs to be burning before they even know we're there."

"Have we got enough bombs?" Jacob asked.

Soasa seemed insulted. "More like, have we got

enough targets?" she remarked.

"Oh, we have plenty of those," Rommond said. He ran his finger across the map of the city, pointing out several areas marked with a red X in a circle. "These are all priority targets once the main armoury is taken out. Their barracks is on the eastern side of the city, but that could easily wait until last, as we won't be mounting a ground assault until we clear out all of their vehicles. All four gates are heavily guarded, but I've sent a message to some of our supporters in the city. Ebronah will pay off as many guards as possible, and the Guild of Brick and Mortar is poised to strike on the ground once we've established air superiority."

"Air superiority is one thing," Jacob said. "The Regime is thick on the streets."

"We will have to make do with what we have."

"What about allies? Is there no one we can call on?" Jacob asked.

"We have no allies," Rommond grumbled.

"What about General Leadman in Copperfort?" Taberah suggested.

"He's no ally. He capitulated very early in the war. It's the only reason the Regime leaves Copperfort alone. Leadman is part of the Resistance only in name."

"But people there quietly oppose the Iron Emperor," Taberah said.

"Yes, quietly," Rommond replied. "We've had enough of that over the years. It's time we got louder."

"What do you want me to do?" Mudro asked, waving his hand over the map as if he could make the entire city disappear. "I could deploy some decoys around the city. We could lure them out."

"I don't want to lure them out," Rommond said. "I want them to burn *in* the city. I want everyone there to see them burning. I want the people there to see their captors in flames. I want the entire city to know what Hell they have been living in."

"What about the everyday folk?" Jacob wondered.

Rommond looked at him as if he were a new recruit. His eyes were stern. "Let me be frank. We are aiming at military installations, but there *will* be civilian casualties. That is unavoidable."

"But won't that turn people against us?"

"Us?" Taberah asked with a smile. "So you've finally joined us?"

Jacob stuck out his tongue and cocked his head.

"Some will turn against us, sure," Rommond replied, "but they have lived under the iron rule of the Regime for many years now, and I am sure they will appreciate their chance for liberty, even if it comes at a cost."

"I lived there for years," Jacob said. "Hell, all my life. It was a scum-filled city even before the Regime came. People have kind of gotten used to that. People just get on with things, get on with life."

"Perhaps, but if we don't do something soon, there won't be much life left in humanity to get on with."

"What if we fail? What if the people don't want to be saved?"

Rommond's eyes were grim. He slammed his hand down on the map, like an explosion from a tremendous bomb. "Then we will burn this city to the ground."

With targets selected, plans were put in motion for the best attack route, and the lieutenants began preparations with Soasa and Alakovi for the deployment of bombs. Rommond returned to his quarters, but Taberah followed him before he had time to shut the door.

"Make this quick," the general said.

"Why didn't you tell me about the bomb?"

Rommond gritted his teeth. "Close the door, and lower your voice."

She closed the door, but she did not lower her voice. "Why didn't you tell me?" she asked again.

"If you were still in the Resistance, you might have known."

"You told me about other things, other projects."

"This was different," he said, with a pause. He sat down at his desk, where an array of guns were scattered. It was rare to see his workspace so untidy. He began cleaning up.

"After all we've been through, you should have told me."

Rommond looked up at her. "And why didn't you tell me about Domas? About Brogan?"

Taberah looked away. "I'm a good listener," she said. "Sharing is another thing entirely."

"Then maybe you will forgive me keeping my own secrets."

"But this isn't your personal little secret, Rommond. This is about the bigger picture. I should be *in* that bigger picture."

"I didn't tell you, because ... because I was ashamed."

"Why?" she asked.

"I made it after Brooklyn died. He wouldn't have approved."

"He's dead," she said. "He can't disapprove now."

"Oh, but he can. His remonstrations haunt me from beyond the grave."

"You never were one to believe in ghosts."

"No, but you were," the general said. "Wasn't that what the Ghostchaser was all about?"

Taberah turned away. "You said we'd never call it that again."

"The Silver Ghost then."

"I don't want to discuss that."

"So maybe the dead haunt us all."

"There are few living left to haunt," she said.

"And there might have been none at all if I had completed that bomb."

"Why did you make it in the first place?"

Rommond's shoulders sagged. "To end this war."

"At all costs?" she asked.

"At all costs."

Taberah sat down. "How big would the blast have been?"

"I don't know for certain," he said. "The aim was to destroy Ironhold in one go. The scientists and engineers did all the calculations."

"Where are they now?"

"Most of them were annoyed when I cancelled the project."

"Let me guess," Taberah said. "They joined the

Armageddon Brigade."

"Yes."

"Well maybe with that knowledge they can finally achieve their aim."

"Let's hope not."

Taberah adjusted in her seat. "Rommond, I know you may think even less of me if I say this, but I have to speak my mind."

"You always have. It is one of the things I value about you."

"Well," she said, "that bomb isn't like you. Many innocent people would have died. Who knows what effect it would have had on our world. Why in God's name did you even contemplate it?"

The shadows gathered on Rommond's face, veiling his features. "The thought had crossed my mind," he said, "that in order to save this world from Hell, I might have to become the Devil."

"And what changed your mind?" she asked.

He sighed a terrible sigh. "I'm not so sure I have."

Chapter Ten

THE SMOG THAT SHIELDS

The Skyshaker sailed closer to the city of Blackout, and though it was nightfall, the city's fumes funnelled high above the buildings like a darker night. The desert sands, which were an enemy to any ground assault, posed no threat to the airship, but Rommond expected a fierce fight for the airways.

They approached the city, where they could make out the silhouette of the domes and spires, of the many chimneys and flumes, of the ramparts and rooftops. A dark, grimy haze, a mix of green and brown, grey and black, hung over the city streets, turning and churning slowly, like a grim broth stirred by some sorcerer in the sky.

In crusader mode, the steel walls and glass windows protected the crew from the toxic fumes, but everyone inside felt a little smothered anyway, like any visitor to Blackout would. The vapour rose in such thick plumes that it almost seemed alive, a creature made by a city's waste, by a city's long neglect, by its industrial greed.

The Skyshaker drifted slowly, hugging the clouds for cover, dimming or dousing its lamps and lights, mimicking as much as possible the silent run of the Lifemaker. Yet sound was not the real enemy in Blackout; it was sight, and so the crew did everything they could to stick to shadows, to pull the veil of night across them like a blanket, and so hide from the city's many watchful eyes.

Sentries were posted in wooden towers a mile in either direction of Blackout, but Cantro easily avoided these, rising as high as he could in crusader mode, which forced the gondola to dock with the balloon. The city itself had numerous large spyglasses posted on its walls, almost large enough, and with high enough magnification, to see what vessels might sail between the stars. But these too were vulnerable to cloud and night, and the city's own noxious gloom.

The atmosphere aboard the airship was tense. This was the first time in years that the Resistance was truly on the offensive, and Rommond knew well that when it came to breaching a castle, the defender always had the upper hand. Though much preparation had been made over the prior two weeks, everyone knew that they were facing almost insurmountable odds.

The Skyshaker began its slow, steady descent from the clouds. Though it could fly high, it needed to fight low, low enough to see its targets clearly, or risk bombing everything and everyone down below. With many people already buying into the Regime's propaganda, the last thing the Resistance needed to do was burn Blackout's citizens alive.

The faint colours of hot air balloons were now visible in the distance, mimicking in their crowded numbers the sprawling cityscape below. Though the smog still disguised them, it was clear that they were numerous, and Rommond's intel from the ground suggested they were even more plentiful than his own lieutenants believed. The battle for Blackout might instead by a war of the heavens.

The city bustled like normal, sending up a clamour to match the clouds. Lights pierced through the gloom, and the Treasury continued to prosper on land, and anywhere else it sunk its golden claws.

"The Treasury taxes these airways," Taberah pointed out.

"Well don't look at me," Jacob said. "I'm skint."

"I've got plenty," Rommond said, as he span the barrel of his revolver.

"The direct approach?"

"None better."

An elaborate hot air balloon, richly adorned, and bearing the golden seal of the Treasury, two interlocking stars, one upright and one reversed, appeared from the smog above the city. In the basket was a guard, who guided the balloon until it almost crashed into the Skyshaker. He banged his fist, with its many golden rings, on one of the airship's windows. Cantro opened it with the flick of a lever.

"Have you got clearance?" the guard bellowed, as the wind tried to steal his voice.

"I'm here to meet an old friend," Rommond said, stepping up to the window.

"That doesn't answer my question," the guard replied. "Do you have clearance?"

"Let me find my papers."

"If you don't have clearance, I'll have to alert the Grand Treasurer. Taxes are double then."

"Here it is," Rommond said, taking out his gun.

Before the guard had time to respond, the general fired, and the man collapsed inside the basket, and the balloon began to drift of its own accord.

"Reel that in," Rommond ordered. "We don't want the Grand Treasurer looking for his taxes just yet."

"With a war going on," Jacob commented, "you'd imagine taxes would be the least of anyone's worry."

"The Treasury are old dogs," Rommond said. "They're fairly predictable."

Grappling hooks were fired across to the Treasury balloon, which was pulled in close to the Skyshaker, filled with additional helium, and then let ascend swiftly into the sky. All the while the airship continued its own gentle drift, as Rommond's lieutenants tried to see through the fog to the military targets mentioned first on the bombing list.

"Eh, Rommond," Taberah said, pointing a finger at a series of giant guns perched on the rooftops just ahead. Their barrels were bigger than the cannons on board the Skyshaker, but these were mechanised, operating via a series of cogs and levers. They swivelled into place, aiming straight at the airship.

Just as Rommond was about to shout an order to turn around, or to abandon ship, the guns fired in unison, but they did not fire bullets or rockets or cannonballs. They fired a thick, dark smoke, which filled the sky swiftly until Cantro could not see where he was steering, and the crew could make out little of the city below.

"Well, that's a new trick," Jacob said.

Taberah moved from window to window. "We can't see a thing."

"That is quite a gamble," Rommond said. "What if I didn't care what my bombs hit?"

"But you do, right?" Jacob asked.

"I do, yes."

"Then I guess that's what makes them the Treasury. They gamble to win."

"We'll play their game then," Rommond said. "Let's play an ace."

"What's that?" Jacob wondered.

Rommond smiled. "You."

Chapter Eleven

DROP

"You were born in Blackout, right?" Rommond asked.

"Born, bred, worked, and wept there," Jacob replied. "Why do I get the impression I'll die there too?"

"Your mission is simple," Rommond said, handing him a Regime uniform. "Perhaps too simple for a smuggler of your calibre."

Jacob raised an eyebrow. "So he says before sending him to his doom. What is it then? What's the mission?"

"You've got to turn those smog guns off."

"Oh, is that all?" Jacob asked derisively.

"They'll likely be guarded."

"So I just need to dig my way through a thousand guards. Got a shovel?"

"There are rebels down there," Rommond revealed. "People just waiting for the opportunity to take back over the city. The Guild of Brick and Mortar is where you'll find them. They will help."

"And how will I know who is who?"

Rommond paused. "Whistler will go with you."

"I will?" Whistler said, with a hint of glee.

"So I can tell the humans from the demons," Jacob said, "but what about the evil humans from the good ones, or the good demons from the evil ones?"

"I'll let you wrestle with that," Rommond replied. "But Jacob, as far as I'm concerned, all of those demons down there are evil."

"I'll go too," Soasa said. "You'll need someone to blow up those guns."

"Fair enough."

Taberah stepped forward. "I think I should go as well."

"No," Rommond said. "No more. The more we send, the more likely we'll be caught."

"I'm starting to feel like an invalid," Taberah griped. "You do know I was faking birth back then?"

"If you want to be useful, Tabs, send down the Ghost."

"I will," she said. "I'll lead the mission."

"No, you won't," Rommond said. "Are you trying to kill that baby of yours?"

Her hand instinctively clutched her belly. She appeared annoyed and embarrassed that it did. Perhaps in her eyes she thought it would be better to clutch a gun instead.

"After everything I did to get the Silver Ghost, I think I deserve to drive it."

"After everything *you* did?"

"I'm not forgetting you or Brooklyn's part in it."

"It seems you are."

"Nothing will make me forget those days, Rommond. Nothing."

The silence that followed was broken by Rommond's lieutenants, who argued over the best way to deploy the Silver Ghost. Some wanted to land the Skyshaker, but Rommond opposed this, as it would almost certainly alert the guards in the many outposts.

"What about a drop?" Taberah asked.

"Not here. We're too close to the city. The smog doesn't make them completely blind." Rommond turned to Cantro. "Pull us back to drop distance. And bring us higher. When we leave this smog, we need to be out of eyeshot."

Cantro turned the Skyshaker around and flew it back, not the way they had come, which Rommond assumed was now being watched, but thirty degrees off from this.

"That's far enough," the general said.

Jacob and his smuggling team clambered aboard the Silver Ghost. Before Soasa closed the door, Taberah grabbed her by the collar. "Bring this back safely," she said. "The Hopebreaker is Rommond's baby. This is mine."

Whistler looked to the floor, and Jacob could not help but think: *What about the one inside you?*

"I'll only blow up the enemy," Soasa quipped, before slamming the door shut.

The warwagon seemed different than it was before. With only three people inside, it felt very odd. There were no gaslights lit, no candles burning. It almost felt abandoned, unloved.

They got dressed quickly, donning their new disguises. It felt odd to wear the uniforms of their enemy. They only hoped it would not somehow change them.

"How do I look?" Jacob asked Soasa.

"Like a demon."

"A pretty demon though, right?"

"Just a demon."

"This uniform's too big for me," Whistler protested. The sleeves covered most of his hands, and the trousers gathered at his shoes, which shined with a gleam typical of the Regime's most orderly forces. It made a marked contrast to the boy's usual frayed and tattered attire.

"You'll grow into it," Jacob said.

"How long is this mission going to be?" Whistler shrieked.

"Relax kid, we'll be in and out in a jiffy."

"Will they really believe I'm a soldier?" the boy wondered.

Jacob wondered it as well.

"I wouldn't worry about that," Soasa said. "Any of their children born here through human parents are, at most, sixteen years old. They're trained young. This is why the war needs to be won soon, or today's children become tomorrow's reinforcements."

"Okay," Jacob said. "Let's get this show on the road. I'll drive." He tried to find the driver's seat, but every door seemed to open into a bedroom.

"Did you not hear what Taberah asked?" Soasa said. "She wanted it back in one piece."

"Fair enough," Jacob said, reminded of his flight from Blackout in the steamtruck. "I'll break something else then."

"There's plenty of smog guns in Blackout to

break."

"What will I do?" Whistler asked.

Jacob smiled at him. "Sit tight, kid."

"Umm, is that all?"

Jacob sat down and placed his boots upon a table, and folded his arms behind his head. "Until we get to Blackout, that's all I'll be doing."

But he was wrong.

A hatch beneath the Skyshaker opened with a clang, and the wind swept into the cargo bay like an invasion. Soasa climbed a ladder in the centre of the vehicle, which led into a one-person cockpit, with a small raised roof, from which she could peer over the silver hull of the warwagon. She put it into gear and revved the engines. It was only at that moment that Jacob asked the question in his mind: *How do we get down to the ground?*

The Silver Ghost rolled forward, down a ramp, picking up speed as it went. The chimneys spat out soot like disgruntled smokers. Then the warwagon slipped through the hole and began to plummet towards the ground.

Inside, Jacob and Whistler clung to their seats, while Soasa clung to the wheel. Jacob peered out of the window, but all he saw was the night sky whisk by. The stars seemed like streaking comets as the Silver Ghost hurtled towards the earth like a meteor of its own.

"I hope you know what you're doing, Soasa," Jacob called up to her, his voice jittering as the vehicle continued its swift descent. He was partly glad the Skyshaker was up so high; the longer the fall, the longer Soasa had to work her magic. Another part of him had a different thought: the longer the fall, the harder the landing. He doubted they would survive that drop at all.

"I've got it," Soasa barked back to him. "Don't worry."

Jacob's apprehension, which was only a fraction of that evident on Whistler's panicked face, lowered just a little, until Soasa's next word struck his ears.

"Damn," she said.

"What is it?" Jacob asked, jumping up several rungs of the ladder. He peered his head into the cockpit, spying Soasa's boots, as she frantically moved about the tiny room.

"It's jammed."

"What is?"

"The parachute."

"Hell," Jacob blurted, before darting up the rest of the ladder and squeezing into the cockpit. "What deploys it?"

"This," Soasa said, pointing to a lever behind him. He turned around on the spot, brushing against her. He was almost pushing buttons on the other side.

He grabbed the lever and tried to pull it down.

"No! Up!" Soasa cried.

He tried pushing it up, but it would not budge. He felt the vehicle plummet even more, and his heart went with it.

"It's jammed," he said, pushing it once more.

"I know it's jammed. Use some force!"

He tried to move back a little so that he could put his shoulder into it, but he could not budge with

Soasa there. "There's no room!" he shouted.

"Let me try," Soasa said.

"Let's try together," Jacob suggested, and they shimmied around a little more, until both of them stood face to face, almost cheek to cheek. At any other time, he would have smiled at her, and made some quip, but there was no time for that. They grabbed the lever together and pushed it up. It moved a little, but not enough. They tried again, but it slipped back down to where it was before.

"Guys!" Whistler cried from down below.

They all knew then that the ground was fast approaching.

Jacob and Soasa glanced once more at each other. It was a fleeting look, but they both knew that it might be their last. *What a way to die*, Jacob thought. In that glance, they communicated to each other the dire necessity of giving their all, or giving their life. The countdown was quick. One, two, three. Push. They shoved with all their might, all their strength, fuelled by their fear, fed by the frenzy of self-preservation. Their muscles bulged. Their veins popped. The superhuman strength they mustered, the demonic fortitude they summoned, was like only that a mother finds when lifting a landship to rescue her trapped child.

The lever snapped into place, and the parachute deployed, catching in the wind and tugging them up, before letting them down slowly.

All three of them breathed a collective, and very audible, sigh of relief. Jacob and Soasa breathed theirs into each others faces. Then they were aware of just how close they stood, body to body, face to face.

"Cosy," Jacob remarked.

"Too cosy," Soasa replied. "I think you should get back down."

Jacob smiled as they shimmied around once more until he could feel his foot near the ladder. He climbed down to find Whistler standing there with his arms crossed.

"You left me here," he said.

"Eh, there's wasn't exactly room for three up there."

"I could have helped."

Jacob looked at the boy's scrawny arms. "This next job, kid, is where you really shine."

Chapter Twelve

LIVING CONTRABAND

The trio left the Silver Ghost on the outskirts of Blackout, hiding in the night shadows, and they began the careful trek towards the city walls. They kept low, like serpents in the sand, winding their way closer, flitting from rock to rock, from cactus to spindly bush, like scurrying desert spiders. In time they fell under the shadow of the immense walls, where Jacob began to search for the many cracks and crevices the city's smugglers used.

"Quick," he whispered when he found one.

They lined up outside the thin passage.

"You've got perhaps the most important job here," Jacob said, looking at Whistler. "Are you ready for this?"

Whistler bit his lip. "No."

Jacob chuckled. "Me neither. I've never been ready for anything in my life."

"I am," Soasa said, opening her coat to show the many sticks of dynamite attached to her belt. All they needed was a fuse. In many ways, she was it.

"We have to do this quietly," Jacob said. He could not help but expect her to go in all guns blazing, or all bombs exploding. She would have made a terrible smuggler.

"That's your job," Soasa said. "I'll let you do quiet and get us in. I'll do loud when we're inside."

"Just … try not to light any fuses as we squeeze inside. It's a tight fit."

"Hey, blowing up the wall is one way to get into the city."

"Yeah, just … not when we're inside the wall."

They sidled through, glad that they lived on rations, for the passage was so thin at points that they virtually had to dig their way through. Soasa was left in the rear, so that Jacob could clear a larger passage for her explosive cargo.

When they emerged inside the city, they found no one around, not even the usual seedy types that skulked about in Blackout's darkest corners. This was worrying. If even the crooks were in hiding, news of Rommond's arrival must have been spreading fast. Everyone in Blackout had seen the posters of the general. *Monster*, they called him. *Madman*, they said. Now they knew the mad monster had grown his demonic wings.

"Okay, kid," Jacob whispered, "keep your eyes peeled."

Whistler looked about frantically, eyes darting to every shadow and every glimmer of gaslight. The fog was low in the city, masking even the pavement up ahead. Who knew what armies, what soldiers, what machines of war, lurked within.

Jacob took out his map. Rommond had marked it in several locations. Some were safe houses. Some were dummy markings, in case Jacob was captured, or the map was lost. Though this was his city, Jacob felt like a stranger, like an invader. This was not just simple smuggling; it was sabotage. The stakes were higher, and the Regime was playing with the Treasury on its side.

"Okay, we'll rendezvous with the Guild of Brick and Mortar," Jacob suggested. "Rommond said they're virtually all part of the Resistance. We can count on them for support."

"I'm counting only on what I've got stuffed inside my coat," Soasa said, "and a good match."

They made for the winding streets. Ducking and dodging was one thing; it was quite another to march up those pathways in the enemy's attire, heads held high, limbs not quivering. Jacob was used to walking straight into the nest of vipers, but with him was a nervous boy, and a walking bomb.

They did their best to blend in, emerging from the smog into the city's crowds, many of whom made for their lodgings, with the frequent cry of "invaders!" and a less frequent pointing to the sky. The trio received a few salutes from Regime soldiers, who urged the citizens to go indoors, and began their new patrols of the city's winding streets. This put Jacob on edge. He could have smuggled better if they did not know they were coming. He was thankful, at least, that most eyes looked to the sky instead.

They followed the route to the headquarters of the Guild of Brick and Mortar, appropriately disguised as a masonry shop. The lights were dim inside, but from the window Jacob could see figures moving back and forth inside.

At last, he thought. *Someone on our side.*

He pushed the door open, which rang a bell. The people inside, three men and two women, stopped suddenly what they were doing. The smugglers entered the shop, and silence entered with them. It was almost like a stand-off. Jacob was not surprised. The last thing allies of the Resistance wanted to see was Regime soldiers barging inside.

"Evening," one of the guildsmen said while tilting his cap.

A fine night for cake and wine, Jacob thought. That was the catchphrase, the codewords, the password to let them know who they were. Yet Jacob did not say it. Something told him to wait.

"Close enough to night at this stage," he said instead. "Still open?"

"Just about to close," the guildman said while loosening his collar. His face was beaded with sweat, as if he had just come in from a hard day's work, but his apron was pristine clean.

Whistler tugged gently on Jacob's arm. "Demons," he whispered.

Hell, Jacob thought. *What do we do now?* He wondered if Rommond knew, if these were sympathisers with the Resistance's cause, but he thought it unlikely that the general would trust them. If nothing else, it would defeat the purpose of sending Whistler.

"We're doing a sweep of the area," Jacob said, feeling the sweat forming on his own brow, feeling the urge to adjust his own collar. "We're urging everyone to stay indoors."

"No worries there, officer."

Jacob was amused; he did not even know his rank. He gave a salute, and turned sharply for the door. Soasa and Whistler followed clumsily. Jacob hoped they would be mistaken for new recruits, and hoped their uniforms did not say otherwise.

As soon as they got outside, and out of earshot of anyone around, Jacob cast off his hat and stamped his foot in frustration.

"Damn it," he said. "So the Regime infiltrated them too. Hell, they're everywhere." He sighed. "Looks like we're on our own down here."

"Good," Soasa replied. "Then we won't have anyone else breathing down our necks."

Jacob shook his head. "We'll have the whole city doing that."

Chapter Thirteen

THE BLACKEST STREETS

They continued towards their objectives, abandoning the city's many safe houses, which were no longer safe. The shadows were a sanctuary now, as were the steam and smog. No matter how much they tried to blend in, it was always better not to be seen at all.

"You were born here?" Soasa asked as she looked about the streets in disgust.

"Yes," Jacob said. "Born and raised. Well, born anyway."

"It's a Hell-hole," she replied, spitting on the ground.

"Perhaps, but it's my kind of Hell-hole."

"The smog," she said with a cough. "It's so thick it's almost solid. It's bad enough putting up with Mudro's leaf. How did you stick this?"

"It isn't so bad," Jacob said. "You get used to it."

"Sure," Soasa replied. "You get used to it when you're dead."

They passed by a series of Wanted posters pasted to the walls of the narrow streets. Several of them were of Rommond, labelled *War-monger* and *The Savage Hawk*, and several more were of Taberah, dubbed *Cult-leader* and *The Stinging Scorpion*; one was of the now deceased Lieutenant Tradam, labelled *The Hawk's Right Talon*, and another was of Mudro, dubbed *The Sorcerer*. Other posters showed figures that Jacob could not recognise. At one time, when he walked or skulked through those streets, he did not even recognise Rommond or Taberah, and did not care. Those days were simpler, but they were still evil days.

"Thankfully we're not up there," Jacob said.

"We're not big enough fish," Soasa replied.

"Hard to be a smuggler otherwise."

Soasa began to rip down the posters of Taberah, scrunching them up and casting them aside. Whistler joined in quickly, tearing down the posters of Rommond and Mudro. He seemed to enjoy this little act of rebellion. At another time, Jacob might have too.

"Come on," he urged them. "Let's leave these. We can deal with them another time, when Blackout is liberated."

"It's a matter of principle," Soasa said.

"And nothing more?"

"Nothing more."

A torch flashed in their direction, and they looked to find a guard standing further down the alley. "You!" he shouted. "Stop that now!"

Soasa threw a smoke bomb in the guard's direction, before charging off. Jacob and Whistler ran after her, turning corner after corner, despite Jacob urging her to slow down and take a different turn. In time they ended up in a dead end, barely illuminated by one of the dim gaslamps.

"Damn it," Jacob said. "This isn't your city, Soasa. You should be following me."

She looked at him defiantly, as if that would never happen.

"Should we head back?" Whistler asked.

But it was too late for that, for they heard the hurried footsteps of the guard in pursuit. He turned that final corner, knowing well that it was a dead end, that he would find the culprits of the vandalism there, but he did not expect to find them armed with guns. His torch flashed in their direction, just enough to see the grim face of Soasa, and the barrel of her pistol, and the brief flash as the gunpowder ignited, followed by a thicker darkness.

The body slumped to the ground before them, and the torch rolled away, stretching and compressing their shadows, as if they were puppets to a god of light. The guard's own shadow hid the growing pool of blood.

"Hell," Jacob said. "That's one way to end up on a poster."

"I'll pose for mine myself," Soasa said while cocking her chin.

"You wouldn't make a good smuggler. Bodies tend to attract attention."

"Can we go?" Whistler pleaded. This clearly was not the kind of adventure he was looking for. *Hell*, Jacob thought, *it's not the kind I wanted either*.

The echo of the gunshot had not fully faded, and it was already punctuated by the sound of approaching footsteps. *An army*, Jacob wondered, but the patter was not enough for that. They braced themselves, and Jacob urged Soasa to wait before firing her gun again, and drawing even more attention to them.

Then a figure charged around the corner, a figure in heels. When she stepped out of the shadows, panting from the pursuit, Jacob was stunned by her beauty. She had immaculate blonde hair, which fell upon her shoulders in perfect waves. She wore a slim white nurse's uniform, with a white hat to match. On it was the emblem of the Regime: a black square on a red cross. She carried a first aid kit, larger than any Jacob had ever seen, and yet she did not struggle.

Whistler tugged on his arm. "She's one of them," he whispered.

A demon.

The nurse saw the guard bleeding and moaning on the ground, and she ran to him, but Jacob seized her arm.

"So," he said, blocking her way. "Off to rat on us?"

She looked him up and down in disgust. "If anyone's a rat here, it's you."

He shrugged. "All of Blackout's kind of like the sewers."

"Let me tend to the wounded."

"Or what?"

"Or he dies, you fool! Do you not care?"

"He's a demon," Soasa said. "Like you."

The woman turned to her. "You're all the same."

Soasa scoffed. "And you're not?"

"So, you're a nurse," Jacob noted. "Can't say we're all that keen on seeing Regime soldiers nursed back to health."

"I don't care who they work or fight for," the nurse replied. "I care that they're wounded."

"Well, that emblem on your uniform kind of tells a different story."

"I have to wear that here. Besides, what's that on yours?"

Jacob covered up the badge sewn into his shirt, suddenly ashamed. "It's a disguise."

"Well," the nurse replied. "You could say mine is too."

"You're skin is," Soasa hissed. "You wear it almost like a real human too."

The nurse sighed. "Nothing I say is going to make you listen. But please, let me help that man."

"He's not a man!" Soasa shouted. Jacob urged her to lower her voice.

"I don't see all these distinctions you make," the nurse replied. "I've tended people on both sides. To me, the only distinction is: alive or dead. I only want there to be one of those."

"Okay then," Jacob said. "Sew 'im up."

"Are you mad?" Soasa objected. "Sew his mouth up."

And yours, Jacob thought. *Who would have thought her voice would be like dynamite as well?*

"It can't hurt," Jacob said.

Soasa shook her head violently.

"What if it was me?" Whistler asked her. "Would you let me die?"

"You're not the same as them," she protested.

"I'm close enough."

"Fine then," Soasa said, folding her arms.

The nurse gave a forced, polite smile. "Thank you."

Soasa ran over to the guard before the nurse got there, and began rummaging through his pockets and belongings. "No radio," she said. "Just checking."

"You'll be looting the dead next," the nurse said.

Soasa cocked her head. "Maybe I'll be looting you."

While the nurse tended the man, removing the bullet and sealing up the wound, Soasa urged Jacob not to trust the woman in white. She might have been a demon, but in that bleached uniform, and with those golden locks, which glistened more than Jacob's dirty blonde, she looked more like an angel.

"We can't kill someone who's trying to save lives," he whispered.

Soasa did not seem as disturbed by the notion, but the presence of Whistler seemed to tame her a little. She put away her gun, but she took out rope instead. As soon as the nurse had cleaned up the guard's wound, she bound and gagged them both, and left them back to back.

"Hell, Soasa," Jacob said, "you can't leave a woman tied up in a shady corner like this. God knows what someone will do to her."

"God knows what I'd do otherwise," Soasa said through gritted teeth. "She's not a woman anyway. In the world they came from, they probably didn't even distinguish between the sexes. It was probably all a blur of tentacle and tail."

The nurse rolled her eyes. She would have said

something if her mouth had not been muffled. She did not fight her bonds. Now that the guard had been treated, she seemed content to simply sit and wait.

"Besides," Soasa continued, tapping the guard with her foot, "she's got company."

There was little time for arguments, and they had already lost much time on their important mission, so they headed back the way they came, Soasa reluctantly following Jacob as he led them around a different street, one he knew would not have tempting posters to tear from the ever-crowding walls. They were entering a richer part of the city, where the lights were that much brighter, the windows cleaner, and the doors locked firmly shut.

"Let's keep our noses down," Jacob whispered. "We need to get through here to the Coal Quarter."

They strolled through the Gold Quarter, which had many guards and many patrols, but few batted an eyelid at them, for eyes were still fixed on the skies, where a growing number of Treasury balloons were rising.

As they walked, Jacob pointed to the two-way radio strapped to Soasa's belt. "How come we don't use them more often?" he whispered, tipping his hat and smiling at a passing patrol. "They would have been handy in the raid on the Hope factory."

"They're a last resort."

"Why?"

"Because all radio frequencies are monitored by the Regime. As soon as we use these, we alert them to our location, and to our plans."

"Ah."

"So, yeah, if you hear a voice come through here," Soasa said, tapping the radio, "it might as well be the voice of the Iron Emperor himself."

They entered the Coal Quarter, which required no announcement. Whatever sign posts there might have been were buried in piles of dirt, and whatever people there were to ask for directions were covered in soot and dust. This was the darkest and dreariest part of the city, the worker's quarter, where the dilapidated buildings huddled together as if for warmth. It was the part that produced the vast majority of the smog that gave the city its most appropriate name.

As soon as they entered the area, they saw the workers toil, and the beggars beg. The latter would have begged in the richer parts of the city, but they quickly learned that the poor give more to the poor than the rich ever do, and they would be hunted from the Treasury Quarter, and maybe even handed in to the Regime to work in the Hope factories, until they could no longer earn their wage of life.

"Why are there so many people on the streets?" Whistler asked.

"There aren't enough houses."

"But there are," the boy objected. "We passed by several boarded up."

"Those were boarded up for a reason."

"Hope-houses," Soasa said. "People get high there."

Whistler looked anxiously at Jacob. "Why?" he asked. "Why make it worse?"

"Sometimes when things are bad," Jacob said, "it seems like they can't get any worse. People are always looking for some kind of relief, no matter how small, no matter how temporary."

"They don't have anything to fight for," Soasa said.

"But they do," Whistler protested. "They've got their lives."

"Sometimes that isn't enough," Jacob said.

They continued through the coal-covered streets, clinging together like the soot clung to the windows. Here and there pale eyes looked out, many eyes from many people huddled together in overcrowded dwellings. The chimneys spewed their toxic waste, the furnaces fired night and day, and the workers hustled to and fro, their clothes and faces blackened by the work.

The beggars reached their scrawny arms up, using whatever strength they had to beg for more. Some lay still, sleeping or dead. Few amo\\\\

ng them spoke, and so they were easier to ignore. Jacob usually avoided this section of the city. They could not afford the amulets, and Jacob could not afford to offer them his pity, for fear that he would feel compelled to do something to help them, yet knowing that there was little he could do.

"Demons!" a man cried, holding up his prayer beads, from which dangled the solar emblem of his god. Few worshipped that deity before the Harvest, and fewer still since. Science had once crushed that religion, but now the new worship of the Iron Emperor crushed it further still.

"They walk among us!" the madman cried. He fawned at Jacob's coat, as if searching for a demon inside the fabric. Jacob reefed it from him and hurried on, but the man followed, calling after him, even, it seemed, calling out his name.

"Don't run, Jacob!" the beggar said. "Don't run from me."

Jacob stopped, as he might have done when he was a child. There was something in that voice, something familiar. He turned to look at the veiled figure, the religious fanatic who seemed to have nothing but his new-found god.

"Who are you?" Jacob asked.

The man pulled down his shawl.

"Father," Jacob cried.

Chapter Fourteen

FINDING FAMILIES

The shock silenced Jacob outwardly, but it created a dozen roaring voices in his mind, the voice of an angry child, of an ignored child, of a child who had to work when others could play. Everything he had locked away came flooding back to him.

"Son!" the man shouted, holding up both his wrinkled hands and reaching forth to touch Jacob's face.

But Jacob recoiled. "Get away from me."

"But son—"

"But nothing. Just … just leave me be."

"Isn't that what I've done? You don't come here. I know you don't. I don't go to the streets you frequent. I let you run your business, and I don't ask for a penny, though I might say that I deserve more than one."

Jacob could not believe his ears. "You deserve money from me?" he asked, drawing forth, letting his anger slip through his gritted teeth.

Soasa grabbed him and tried to pull him back. "We don't have time for this," she said. "We have a mission."

Jacob's father held up his prayer beads to Soasa's face. "I have a mission too!" he bellowed. "And everyone must hear it, that we might be cleansed of sin, the sin that brought upon us this ruin."

"No," Jacob said. "You brought your own ruin upon yourself, but that wasn't enough for you. You had to share it with your family. You ran up the debt, and we had to pay for it."

"I didn't mean to," his father said, with tears in his eyes.

Soasa rolled her own. "For God's sake, Jacob, let's resolve this another time."

Yet Jacob would not listen.

"Fine," Soasa said. "I'll do this without you."

She turned and marched off before Whistler could stop her. Whistler remained, urging Jacob to follow Soasa.

"Why did you keep pretending?" Jacob asked his father.

"I had to."

"Why? To save face? That's all you saved."

"I couldn't admit that I was penniless, that I didn't have enough to feed my family, that I wasn't the man I told everyone I was."

"But it was all a lie."

"I know it was a lie, son! I know! Every night I came home, every night I claimed I had another busy day at the factory, I knew that I had gambled, and I knew that the money I gave your mother for food, for the shoes you wore, was borrowed money, borrowed by the bankers, by those men who'd break your knees if you didn't pay it back. And sometimes I got lucky in the races, and I was able to pay them back. But mostly I just ended up with bigger debts."

"Debts *we* had to pay."

"It was either that or it was my life."

"It was *my* life, father," Jacob said. "It was mother's life. That's the interest you paid."

"You can't blame me forever."

"Maybe not, but I can blame you now."

"What can I do to make it up? I don't have any money."

"I don't want money," Jacob said, and he could not help but notice Whistler's fervent gaze. "I thought I did, but I don't. I want my childhood back. I want to be able to go to sleep at night and not have the image of all those toys I could not play with burned into my mind. I want to be able to think of those years before the Harvest and want to return to them, instead of thinking that maybe things are better under the iron rule of the Regime."

"Better with the demons?" his father cried. "They're everywhere, Jacob. Don't trust anyone! Don't even trust me!"

"I don't."

His father did not seem to notice. He was too caught up in his speech.

"They could be anyone," he continued, pointing a finger at Whistler. "*He* could be one of them!"

"He's not," Jacob barked, as Whistler looked to his feet.

"But they walk among us, son. They've gotten under our skin!"

His father ran his prayer beads all over his body, as if fighting off some demon infestation.

"You know what, father, just go," Jacob said.

"But I've nowhere *to* go."

Jacob shook his head. "I don't care. I'm not your keeper. Hell, when I was a kid, you clearly weren't mine."

"The Lord forgives me, son. Will you not forgive me too?"

"I'm no god. It's not that easy for me."

Jacob began to walk away, but his father followed.

"The Lord looks out for me now. He can look out for you too!"

Jacob walked faster, and Whistler struggled to keep up. Jacob's father struggled more, and in time he could no longer match his son's fervent pace. When Jacob could no longer see his father waving his hands madly in the background, he stopped and sighed.

"Where's Soasa?" he asked.

"She went off," Whistler told him. "She's going to find the smog guns alone."

"Damn," Jacob said. "She doesn't know this city."

"She'll get lost," Whistler said.

Jacob thought that too, but he also thought that she might find the barrel of a different gun.

Chapter Fifteen

THE BANKER MOB

Jacob raced after Soasa, changing direction when Whistler called out that she went a different way. He expected to find her in custody, or find her bruised and battered body, or never find her at all. But there she was, running around the streets, drawing little attention.

"Where have you been?" Jacob asked.

"Where've I been?" she said with incredulity. "I've already rigged two of the smog cannons, with no help from you. This isn't exactly the best time to have a family reunion."

"It's not a reunion."

"Whatever," she said, taking out a new stick of dynamite. "It's time we introduce *my* family to the neighbourhood."

They found their way to the largest cannon, perched on the roof of the city's old museum, which now was furnished with artificial artefacts depicting the eternal and glorious reign of the Iron Emperor, as if he had always lived there, as if the invasion had never happened, as if the memories of so many people were of little consequence at all.

They entered the building, which was largely

empty. It was only ever crowded in the mornings, when the tour guides gave their revisions of Altadas' history to the city's young. The lies fell equal on human and demon ears.

"We need to evacuate this site," Jacob told the nearby guards, who saluted and began clearing out the room.

When the place was empty, they headed up to the roof, where they found more guards who were less willing to abandon their posts. A few well-aimed bullets fixed that problem.

"If we can get this out," Soasa said, patting the smog gun, "it should clear most of the sky."

"Apart from the fumes created naturally here."

"Apart from that," Soasa said.

She swiftly unloaded her explosive cargo, and strapped several sticks of dynamite to the barrel of the smog gun. They could have simply turned it off, but Rommond wanted a more permanent solution. Dynamite was pretty permanent.

"Right, that'll do it. This is going to be a big blast, so we need to get far away."

They rolled out the fuse and laid it down the stairs, around the corner, and into the dirt paths below, where Soasa connected it with the fuses leading to the two other guns she had previously rigged. Soasa and Jacob held the tube on either end and walked backwards as they extended the rope to its farthest length, while Whistler immediately ducked for cover.

"Here goes nothing," Soasa said.

She placed the fuse down and reached for her pocket.

"Stand up slowly," a firm voice called out from behind them.

Soasa glanced at Jacob, and he could tell from the look that she was just a fraction of a second away from readying the charge. She began to slowly reach for the fuse, but two bullets whisked by her hand.

"Stand up slowly," the voice said again, "or we'll put some bullets in your legs, and then you'll have an excuse not to stand."

Whistler was the first to stand up and turn around.

"At least there's one brain between the three of you."

Jacob followed suit, and he saw a line of men standing across the street, some of them pointing guns, others holding iron bars and wooden bats. A mere glance showed who they were: Treasury bankers, for they wore the finest black suits with tails, and the one in the centre wore a small top hat, rimmed with gold. Each of them had a golden handkerchief in their top coat pocket, and the golden chain of a pocket watch hung from their trouser pockets—a watch to tell them when to collect a debt.

Soasa eventually turned around, but she would not hold up her hands.

"You're Rommond's lot, aren't you?" the banker asked, patting the bat against his hand. They knew well that he would not be so gentle when he was patting them on the kneecaps.

"Never heard of him," Jacob replied.

"Really?" the banker said. "By your accent, you're a Blackout boy. You telling me you never saw a poster of the Hawk?"

"I'm not much of a bird-watcher."

The banker turned to his comrades with a grin. "I'm going to enjoy breaking him."

"What do you want?" Jacob asked. "We're just passing through."

The banker laughed, and pointed up to the smog-choked sky. "Like that airship up there is just 'passing through'?"

"No idea. I'm more of a walking kind of guy."

"Well, *soldier*, if you help us bring in Rommond, we'll make sure you can still walk in the morning. You see, he has a debt to pay, and it's a big one."

Jacob shrugged. "As I said, never heard of him."

"If that uniform of yours was real," the banker said, "you'd have a pretty good idea who Rommond is."

"I just do as I'm told," Jacob replied. "Never been told to remember a name."

The banker looked to his comrades with irritation. "Well, I'm telling you what to do now, and I'm telling you to end this pretence."

Jacob shrugged again. "There's nothing to end." Then he had a thought: *Maybe there is. Our lives.*

There was a sudden crackle on Soasa's two-way radio. The voice was muffled, but it was unmistakable: it was Rommond. "Come in, Soasa," the general said. They had delayed too long. He had obviously grown impatient, or worried.

"Kind of busy at the moment," Soasa said through gritted teeth into the radio. Whistler seized the radio from her and cried "Help!" into it, before a banker shot it from his hand.

The main banker smiled as if he had just received a new deposit. "You lot don't exactly value your ability to walk, now, do you?"

"All this talk of broken legs," Soasa said. "I need a smoke."

She took a box of matches from her pocket. The guns pointed in her direction.

"Don't you think there's enough smog in this city?" the banker asked.

"Maybe this will help clear the air."

She struck the match, and held it up.

"Drop it," the banker ordered.

Soasa smiled. "Sure."

She dropped the match, and it sparked the fuse. It wound its way like a snake through the dirt, a little speck of fire consuming every thread of the rope, until it could consume something even bigger.

Soasa held up her arms, joining Jacob and Whistler.

The banker took out his own pistol, and pointed it at Soasa. But before he could shoot, the fuse reached the dynamite planted around the smog cannon behind Soasa, resulting in a monumental explosion that threw her, Jacob, and Whistler forward, and the bankers backwards.

When the dust cleared, and the ringing was no longer heard in their ears, Jacob stumbled up and pulled Soasa and Whistler from the rubble. Even as he did so, he saw many of the bankers stirring from the dirt as well.

Jacob glanced around. He knew that if they ran,

they would likely be gunned down. He reached for his gun, but it was no longer holstered on his belt. He saw it half-buried several metres away. He knew he would never reach it, for the banker mob was already rising, and their guns were well within reach.

The trio raised their hands again. Their mission was successful, but not without cost. The Treasury would either beat them or bargain with them, or likely both. The smiles on the bankers were wide, like the openings of gigantic purses.

The dust cleared upon the ground, and the smog cleared in the sky. Jacob could not help but look up and see the glittering fleet of balloons gathering around the Skyshaker. But there was something else, something smaller that was falling from the sky.

"What the hell is that?" Soasa cried.

Jacob hoped it was not a bomb.

He strained his eyes until he realised that it was the Hopebreaker with a huge parachute, descending from the heavens like an iron angel. He could hear the growing rumble of the engines and the clang of the turret as it swivelled into place.

Backup, he thought.

Chapter Sixteen

THE HAWK HAS LANDED

The Hopebreaker struck the ground, sending up a plume of dust like a mushroom cloud. Rommond rocked inside it, clutching the steering sticks with his hands, and the seat with his legs. He revved the engines and felt the tracks grip the land outside.

"The Hawk has landed," he spoke into his two-way radio.

"Scorpion received," Taberah replied, her voice clipped. Even at this close a distance, the radio frequencies were weak. The Regime had learned to jam them very early on, and if they could not jam them, they could disrupt them, and if they could not disrupt them, they could monitor them. Rommond knew that somewhere in the Iron Emperor's fortress in Ironhold, the city of Blackout was lighting up blue on a map—a map that was to date almost completely red.

"Now," he said. He was not entirely sure if he was talking to himself or to the landship—maybe both. The purr of the engine suggested the landship understood. "Let's hope I can clear this city before the Iron Guard gets here."

He had not intended to land this early, not until

the Skyshaker lived up to its name, but Whistler's plea told him that that the team on the ground was in trouble. That wisecracker Jacob had smuggled them inside, but Rommond would smuggle them out.

He headed for where the ruined smog gun left a rising pillar of smoke, like the souls of the machine spirits rising to the heavens. He drove with such haste that he clipped the corners of buildings as he thundered through the thoroughfare. The mere presence of the Hopebreaker, with its brightly-painted Resistance emblems, scared many of the civilians away, while the few shocked soldiers who dared to fire on it wasted bullets better spent on the trio of saboteurs that Rommond hoped would last just long enough to sabotage again.

He turned the final corner sharply, only to find a Menacer Mark I there, with its crew languishing outside a local bar. They jumped up, grabbing their hats and guns, and raced towards their landship, but Rommond raced towards it faster. Then a Moving Castle stepped out from the street behind the Mark I, and its crew were anything but languishing; their guns were all aimed at the Hopebreaker, with just a second left to fire. Rommond used that second wisely, for he rammed the Mark I with his own landship, and drove it back into the Moving Castle, which collapsed upon its mate. Rommond ignored the crew who tumbled from its crenellations. He had no time for prisoners, and he only took human ones.

He belted down the city's streets, crushing placards, knocking the signs off shops, and he was grateful that, on his arrival, many of the civilians had already barricaded themselves indoors. Yet some were civilians only in name, for many rushed to grab their uniforms and guns. Some of them were just teenagers. When a home city was under attack, everyone became a soldier. Mothers became the generals of families. Homes became barracks or bunkers. The streets became trenches. Every door became the front line.

Rommond turned the final corner leading to the ruins of the smog gun, and saw the troublesome trio resting on those ruins. For a moment he almost thought they were Regime soldiers, and had to take his finger off the trigger. The disguise was almost too good. Demons could pose as humans, but it seemed that humans could do the reverse.

But there were no demons around, no real soldiers running to and fro, no mob bankers waving their infamous bats, and no one tying up Jacob and company, or parading them through the streets.

Rommond halted the Hopebreaker and pushed his head through the hatch.

"What's going on?" he asked. "I thought you were in trouble."

"We were," Soasa told him. "The Treasury's debt collectors almost had us."

"Where are they now?" the general said, looking about.

"I think you rolled over them," Jacob said.

Soasa smirked. "Your little parachute jump was all the distraction I needed."

"So you're not in trouble," Rommond said with a sigh of relief.

Then they heard the rumble of at least a dozen engines, and they quickly saw a convoy of landships and trucks, armed to the teeth, rolling into the street.

"We are now," Jacob blurted.

Rommond ducked inside, and the Regime's roaming arsenal turned to greet him.

"Kill the Resistance!" Jacob shouted, pointing towards the Hopebreaker, and hoping his disguise was still as good as ever.

He fired a token shot at the general's landship, knowing it would bounce off the hull, and hoping it would not accidentally fly through one of the tiny viewports and strike Rommond dead inside. The guns of the Regime's landships swivelled into place, and the gunners had no qualms with bringing down the hawk that had hunted them for years.

Chapter Seventeen

THE GOLDEN HOST

The smog cleared like dispersing clouds, only it did not reveal the probing rays of the sun, for the curtain of night had been drawn tightly shut. Dotted in the sky like stars were dozens of hot air balloons, some large and some small, but all of them lavishly decorated, bearing numerous lanterns, and who knew what they bore for guns.

Taberah watched as the fleeing fog revealed more and more of the Treasury's golden host, and though the Skyshaker would have given the most doubtful person a firm confidence, the growing fleet of balloons eroded hers. She expected resistance, but she did not expect to find so much.

"Damn," she said. Everyone was thinking it. Their only hope was that it might be a collective curse upon the Treasury, and hope that the Treasury was not voicing their own hex in return.

Mudro stepped up beside Taberah. "Let's hope they're decoys."

Yet Taberah knew for certain that they were not.

The Treasury never fired first. They could afford to wait. The balloons were every colour imaginable, but the one colour they all shared was in the trimmings, and it was gold. Bands of the metal wrapped around the balloons, chains of golden coins hung down from the baskets, and some even had large golden emblems stuck to the balloons like targets.

The Skyshaker drifted between them, and the Treasury's golden fleet drew in closer and began to crowd around it. As it did, the large guns inside the baskets became intimately visible. Taberah knew that Rommond's airship could take out half the Treasury's force, maybe even all, but it could not block or dodge every bullet. If the battle started now, the Skyshaker would be its own bomb, falling upon the city of Blackout.

"I think it's time for you to do your magic," Taberah said, turning to Doctor Mudro.

Mudro took a final, slow puff of his pipe, savouring the taste. He raised the pipe to Taberah, then turned and hobbled off hurriedly to the aft of the vessel, where Boulder was panting and laying out a series of uninflated balloons.

"This is a waste," he said.

"They don't cost much."

"A waste of helium."

"I think we've reached our destination," Mudro said.

"I was hoping this wouldn't be our final one."

Mudro did not seem so sure.

"Well," Boulder said, extending his arms to show the assortment he had laid out. "This is everything you stored away. I've counted ninety-five."

"I had a hundred."

"Well, you must have lost them."

"No matter," Mudro said, taking up one of the balloons, which had a wooden gondola attached to it, painted to look like iron. "The exact number isn't that important. What matters is the larger number that is planted in the Treasury's mind."

Boulder assembled his men, who brought in cannisters of oxygen and helium, and began filling up the balloons. Because they were not real airships, and because they were so light, they only needed a fraction of the helium required otherwise, but they needed oxygen to give the balloons mass, the kind of mass that might frighten the enemy.

"We can't send these out yet," Boulder said. "They'll see us launching them."

Mudro was not fazed. "Let Taberah take care of that."

On the ground, the success of Soasa's mission was cut short by a crackle and a muffled voice over the two-way radio. She held it up to everyone's ears, and they squinted and strained their hearing. It sounded like Taberah on the other end.

"Turn back ... the ..."

Soasa shook her head in frustration. "I didn't get that. Say it again."

"... back on ..."

"Is she asking us to get back on the airship?" Jacob postulated.

"Maybe she's telling us to watch our backs?" Whistler suggested.

"One more time, Taberah," Soasa said.

"Turn … on … smog gun."

"Turn back on the smog gun," Whistler said.

Everyone looked up to where the Skyshaker was surrounded by a hundred glimmering Treasury balloons, and then they looked back to the ruins of the smog gun beside them, sending up only a thin stream of smoke from the cinders. If only the dynamite had not worked so well.

Taberah slammed down the two-way radio on the dashboard. She hoped they had received the message. She knew for certain that the Regime had received it too. If the Treasury had not already notified its puppet-master, this was sure to let them know. Taberah knew with grim certainty that the Regime would now send stronger puppets. All she could do was wait, but it often felt that when it came to time, the Iron Emperor still pulled the strings.

Alakovi stormed onto the cockpit of the Skyshaker. "What are we waiting for?" she bellowed. She looked as though she might throw herself through the window and onto one of the enemy balloons, and merely dust off the glass.

"If we fire now, we're done for," Taberah said, turning back to the window, where she could see all those glistening balloons, and all those well-aimed guns.

"It's not like you to wait," the Copper Matron said. Several of her Vixens entered the cockpit and stood beside her.

"Well, sometimes Rommond is right," Taberah said. "*Play your cards on your own time*, he used to say."

Alakovi scowled at her. "One of these days, Taberah, you won't have anything to play."

Chapter Eighteen

HELL IN THE HEAVENS

In the sky above Blackout, the Resistance endured their agonising wait. Alakovi argued with Taberah, and others joined the dispute, until it seemed that Taberah was outnumbered by more than just Treasury balloons. She gave herself a silent deadline. One more minute. One final chance to give Soasa time to get that smog gun working again. Taberah was eager for action, but she was not eager for death. She only hoped that if she gave in to Alakovi's demands, they would not later think of life, and ask: one more minute.

The seconds died, one by one, until there were no more of them to count. Alakovi looked at Taberah, who nodded in defeat. There was no more time for waiting. They had all been through limbo long enough. It was time to go to Hell.

"Here goes nothing," Cantro said, as he prepared to change gears.

"Here goes everything," Taberah replied, and she marched down to the glass dome beneath the front of the airship, where the largest gun with the most plentiful supply of ammunition was situated. She sat down in the leather seat and tapped the glass. She was not sure if it was for luck or if she was testing its fragility. It was almost like the bulging belly of the airship, and it reminded her of her own. How she ached, and she felt an inner ache that was not merely physical. The glass showed the heavens, and the earth far beneath, and the many gunners in the crowding balloons, with the many lanterns illuminating their anxious faces and nervous fingers.

She took a hold of the trigger, and she almost felt like holding her breath. It was now or never. They could no longer wait for events on the ground, and the longer they did, the more likely it was that everyone down there would be caught or killed. It was all or nothing. She knew that she could not do nothing, so she had to give it her all, even if that meant her life, and the life of her unborn child.

She gave the signal, and then she fired, and the other gunners fired in unison, sending a hail of bullets in almost all directions, bar up, where the gods cowered, and bar down, where another battle raged.

Several of the Treasury's hot air balloons went down in the first volley, but there were so many of them, and not enough guns jutting out of the Skyshaker's hull to take them all out. The Treasury, however, could afford plenty of those little iron pellets, which might as well have been money firing from their guns.

Cantro led the airship through in crusader mode, gaining height and gaining speed. The bullets whisked by. The Resistance fired up and down, where balloons appeared seemingly from nowhere, and the Treasury launched an answering fire, a vertical hail, their own metal hate. Each round cost them a tiny fortune, but by God, they would spend it all to stop someone else from taking it from them.

The Skyshaker zig-zagged through the canopy of colours, through the glint of golden adornments, through the dull gleam of gunfire. At times Cantro brought them dangerously close to the balloons, and at other times he bumped straight into them. Rommond had secured the best material for the Skyshaker's outer shell, the envelope that housed several smaller balloons inside, each attached to its own separate air cannisters. The Skyshaker could take some hits, but the question was: how many?

The bullets did not zig or zag, but with so many gunners out there, they might as well have. Cantro found his aerial road blocked by a barrage on many occasions, and at the speed he was going, he could not halt. So he pulled up higher into the sky, or he dived down lower. Yet everywhere he went, the Treasury was there, as if every angry banker had taken to the skies.

Taberah took them out by the dozen. The seat swivelled, and the gun swivelled too, with a thick rubber surround that creaked and whined as she pushed and tugged the gun into place. Mostly she aimed for the balloons, some of which fizzed out and slowly descended, others of which popped and plummeted, but here and there her only shot was the baskets, and the gunners inside them. They were mostly fellow humans, fighting for the side that was quickly wiping them out. Now Taberah was reluctantly doing the same.

Alakovi was in charge at the back of the airship. She armed large missiles, which she fired periodically into a pile of Treasury balloons. Sometimes the explosions hit them directly, and other times the force merely knocked them away. It took much longer to arm and fire these missiles, but they devastated the heavens, and left the evidence of their devastation far below.

What the people on the ground must have seen. Explosions in the sky, dark lines of bullets criss-crossing over one another, and a lightning-fast airship whizzing between them all. The tattered red, yellow, green, and blue balloons fell by the dozen, some draping over the roofs of buildings like a veil of mourning, others gathering in the murky streets, giving them a bit of much-needed colour, at a monumental loss of life.

"We've got this," Taberah called out to her comrades, when it seemed that a patch of the sky was clearing, that they had cut their way through the barrier of balloons. She thought of Rommond far below, waiting for his bombs, waiting to liberate the ground like she had liberated the sky.

Then she heard an angry hiss of air, which seemed louder in the glass dome than it might have done in the deck above. She knew instantly that there was a puncture in the Skyshaker's envelope, that Cantro's skilful dodging was not enough to escape the endless stream of enemy gunfire.

Taberah thought with bitterness that she should not have tempted the fates, not when she was so high up, not when she was so close to them. Yet it was their favour that had let the Resistance survive this long. You either tried and tempted, or you did not try at all.

"We've got a breach!" Cantro called out over the intercom.

They heard the heavy pants of Boulder as he tried to issue a reply.

"Patch it up, Boulder!" Taberah cried. "Patch it up!"

Boulder waddled through the corridors with a speed that almost matched the airship. He threw himself up several rungs of ladders, pushing through hatches until he came to the section just beneath the envelope. He grabbed one of the gas masks in the nearby storage area and hurriedly placed it on as he stepped into the enormous rubber shell that housed the Skyshaker's own treasury of balloons.

The air was thinner there. He could feel it before the gas mask slipped into place. There were two tiny oxygen cannisters attached to the sides of the mouthpiece, just enough for ten minutes of air. *Not enough*, he thought. He was already out of breath before he hauled up his toolkit.

The chamber was very dark, and this might have been an obstacle, were it not for the fact that he could see clearly a beam of light from outside where the puncture was. He hurried over to it, stumbling as he went, grabbing hold of the ropes holding the balloons in place as Cantro continued his aerial acrobatics.

Two other engineers clambered in after him, grabbing gas masks as they went. They helped him hold up a large patch of stiff rubber, which was just big enough to seal the breach.

"Hold that up," Boulder shouted through the gas mask, his voice muffled.

The engineers held the patch in place, but it blocked the incoming light, and the gaslight one of the engineers had brought up with him was too dim. Boulder cursed, and kicked his toolbox when his thick fingers could not find the sealant he was desperately looking for.

Then he heard a stifled shout, and the light shone in suddenly from the even larger rupture in the Skyshaker's outer shell. He saw one of the engineer's slumped on the ground, blood pouring from his head. And he heard a sharp whistle to his left, where two of the inner balloons were pierced, and were now leaking precious helium by the second.

He felt the Skyshaker begin to sink.

"Hold it up!" Boulder shouted to the remaining engineer, and even as he did, several others, even some of Alakovi's Copper Vixens, climbed into the chamber. They donned their gasmasks, and they took up rubber patches and raced to the inner balloons, even as Boulder tried desperately to seal the outer one.

The air filtered out of the airship, and time went with it. Boulder felt his own oxygen reserves running low, as if his own lungs were punctured too. Everything became harder. His body burned. His brow poured. His eyes stung. There was no warning that his ten minutes were up. His symptoms were the only warning he would get.

The patch was put in place, and Boulder began

to apply the sealant around the rim. The goggles that were part of his gas mask began to steam up, and he found it hard to see. By now he was guessing where the sealant should go. For all he knew he could be sealing his own hand.

Damn it if this goes down on my watch, he thought, and he barely had his wits left to think it. He pulled his gas mask off, and he felt the sudden shift in air pressure. He held his breath, and cast his eyes on the remainder of the rubber patch he had left to seal. *Just another minute.*

He did not know if the others had completed their jobs, their frenzied duties, but if he could just seal the outer hull, then any escaping helium from the inner balloons would still be trapped there. The Skyshaker would still have enough buoyancy to support its weight, to let it dip and rise as Cantro needed to avoid another stream of bullets, and another dangerous puncture.

Boulder applied the last of the sealant, and he and his fellow engineers held it in place. It had to hold. If they took their hands away, who knew if it would come away with them. It seemed to be working. The airship rose again, just a little, but it was enough. Everything would be okay.

But Boulder's eyes were growing dark. He could no longer hold his breath. There was nothing left to hold. The darkness seemed a little different then. It was not just the dim of the chamber, which the gaslight could barely illuminate. It was an inner kind of darkness, one that no light could chase away. Boulder collapsed upon the ground, gasping for breath. He had saved the ship's air supply, but he had not saved his own.

Chapter Nineteen

URBAN MAZE

The Regime on the ground fired in unison, as if they had one mind, one mission. They did: kill Rommond, at any cost. The bullets battered off the hull of the Hopebreaker, and though it withstood them, the general did not want to take his chances against missiles and other more dangerous ammunition.

He drove off, with his gunner Tomdan turning the turret as he went. How he wished to have a full platoon at his disposal, to show the enemy what a real army was like.

Tomdan fired at the advancing landships as Rommond led the Hopebreaker away. Several of the enemy vehicles halted in flames, but there were many of them, too many for the shells of a single turret gun.

Rommond drove the Hopebreaker into a narrow alley, just big enough to squeeze through. He knew this would stop some of the larger enemy vehicles from pursuing, but he just hoped they would not find another way around. He had studied the street maps of Blackout for days, but the Regime had ruled that city for years, and they knew it better than he ever could.

"Faster!" Tomdan cried, when he saw several

trucks loaded with explosives, and pumping smoke and steam like their drivers pumped sweat, thundering down towards the Hopebreaker. The fumes they left behind masked the numerous landships that followed in their train.

Rommond gave it everything he had, accelerating as fast he could while still maintaining control. He could not reach maximum speed in an urban environment, not if he wanted to stop and turn, as he often had to do through the city's meandering streets. How he was glad that the people had been warned to stay indoors. If they had not, he was not so sure he could slow down enough in time to save them.

The people were not entirely safe in their homes, however. Shells exploded in buildings close to the Hopebreaker. The Regime did not care if some civilians died, or even if they all did, so long as Rommond's body was found among the ruins. He mused with melancholy on what the Iron Emperor might have done to Blackout if he had access to that same bomb that Rommond had been working on.

"Tabs," Rommond called into the two-way radio. "We could do with a little help here."

There was no response. She was probably busy. He could hear what sounded like a rolling thunder in the heavens, and every so often he saw the ruins of a Treasury balloon collapse into the street. It seemed that she was winning that battle up above. The Treasury could afford to lose it; it had enough money, enough gold and iron, to win the war.

The Hopebreaker left the narrow streets and climbed a mountain of debris in the central courtyard of the city, the same place he had first met the Regime's iron arsenal. Tomdan knew Rommond's tactics well. The general wanted to take out some of the larger guns from behind. Tomdan was more than happy to oblige.

The large, box-shaped landships were almost planted firmly in the ground. Their turrets faced in all directions. The Regime had fought Rommond long enough to know what he might try. They did not expect him to try it so soon, however, and the Regime gunners were not as watchful as they should have been.

Tomdan fired several volleys, which took out four landships before the Hopebreaker ducked into the dingy alleys on the far side. By the time the enemy bullets followed, they caught two of the pursuing trucks instead. The explosion rocked the city and added more bricks and dust to the growing monument of debris in the city centre.

But the Regime was not altogether unwary. Rommond found anti-landship guns placed in several of the smaller streets, primed and ready, and packing a punch that could easily pierce even the Hopebreaker's thick metal hide. He avoided some of these with sharp turns, the kind of turns that many of his older models simply not could make. But the guns spat their lethal venom, which burrowed through the hull at the back of the Hopebreaker, adding more light, and adding more risk, to those inside.

"The fuel tanks," Tomdan called out. They were dangerously close to where the gun holes were. The diesel engine gave Rommond the advantage, but it could also be his doom.

"I know," he grumbled.

He was driving like a madman, crushing everything in his path, cutting corners and even crashing through the edges of buildings. There was no time left for safety, for careful guiding, and no time left for planning. Everything was instinct. There were no actions, only responses.

Rommond barked into the radio. "Tabs, we need some iron rain."

"A little busy up here," Taberah responded, with the sound of gunfire muffling her voice.

Rommond found himself praying silently. He was not sure who he was praying to. He did not believe in the god of the solar cult that had sprung up in the city, or the many pantheons of the tribes that lived in the wilderness. He found he was praying to metal, to iron rivets and copper bolts, to cogs and pistons, to the very tracks and treads that locked and sprung into place as the wheels of the landship span with a religious frenzy. Perhaps, he thought, that he was really praying to the spirits of the machines, like Brooklyn used to.

The chase continued into the night, and though the Hopebreaker destroyed many of its assailants, it seemed that there were always more to replace them. Tomdan had gotten in many lucky shots, but the Regime gunners only needed one, and they had lots of guns, lots of chances.

Then Rommond heard a grunt from Tomdan, and when he glanced to see, the man was slumped on the floor in a pool of blood.

Damn. Rommond knew he could not drive and shoot at the same time. He either let them chase him, and survived, or he took up the gun position, and would likely be gunned down in the process. It was not much of a choice: Flee or Die. Yet sometimes flight felt just as bad as death, if not worse.

"Tabs, get me those bloody bombs!" Rommond shouted into the radio.

No response.

It became a game of cat and mouse, a game Rommond often enjoyed in the early days of the war, when he was the cat. Now he was the Hawk, and he should have been the predator, but he ran and drove like prey.

He glanced through the viewports to the sky above, where the lanterns of the Treasury balloons were one by one blotted out, and where new lights, the light of tremendous explosions, took their place. Dark shapes, and flashing fires, fell from the heavens, like demons and angels hurtling to the ground. It reminded Rommond of the bombs that should be falling, but the bombs never came.

Then something blocked his vision, and everything inside the Hopebreaker went dark. Rommond checked the viewports. He reached his hand through one, hoping it would not get blown off. He felt the fabric of a Treasury balloon. *Of all the places to land*, he thought.

"I need to get out," he said. He had forgotten that Tomdan was dead. The dead did not need to give permission.

Rommond opened the hatch at the top of the

landship and popped his head outside. The balloon covered most of the vehicle. He only hoped it covered it from the view of the Regime. He climbed out and jumped to the ground. The he grabbed the balloon and tried to reef it off his prized landship. He managed to remove some of it, but it was so big and unwieldy, and parts of it were caught on the machinery, that he could not get it loose. Some was even jammed between the treads.

Then Rommond heard the revving of an engine and the pumping of pistons, and he knew that another landship was nearby. He turned his head and saw the turret twisting into place. He knew he had only seconds to react. He ran from the Hopebreaker and dived behind a broken wall, just in time to see the flash of fire, and hear the initial boom, and feel the hail of landship parts fall down upon him.

He had little time to feel. He emerged from the rubble, checked himself for serious injuries, and glanced about. The haze of dust, and the dirt lodged in his eyes, made it hard to survey his surroundings. He could hear the purring of the enemy landships as they drove by. He peered above the broken wall and saw them driving in almost all directions. Then he saw a truck pull up, and the doors sprung open. A dozen troops hopped out, racing with guns raised to the ruins of the Hopebreaker. Rommond knew what they were looking for. Half the city's posters made it clear. They were looking for him—dead or alive.

He watched for a moment as they hauled Tomdan out, badly burned. They were not gentle with his body. The dead no longer needed pillows. "We got him!" they shouted, cheering to each other, cheering into their radios. "We got the Hawk!"

The posters clearly were not good enough.

Jacob, Soasa and Whistler struggled to get the main smog gun back in working order. Much of it was in ruin, and the metal was still hot, scalding them when they tried to position it in place.

To their surprise, other Regime soldiers came up to help them.

"We need to blind the Resistance," Jacob told them. He was getting good at lying, so good, in fact, that he was frequently blinding the Regime. There was something powerful in those pips upon his shoulders, and those medals upon his chest. Now he knew what Rommond felt, but he felt it deep behind enemy lines.

Supplies were called in, and several engineers began working on the smog gun, tearing out the old cogs and pistons, and putting new ones in. The barrel was half-destroyed, but there was still enough of it left to send up a heavy plume of smoke. It would not be quite as thick as it was before, but it would be enough. The city's own natural smoky skies would do the rest.

As soon as the work was completed, the engineers were called away. There was no end of things to fix. While the city had still not been bombed, Rommond had caused significant destruction in the Hopebreaker alone.

A few soldiers stayed behind to guard the smog gun, which Soasa cranked and aimed at the Skyshaker, giving their comrades their much-needed cover. But

Jacob knew that Taberah would only want the smoke for so long, a brief respite before the bombing truly begun. As soon as the guards turned their backs, he knocked them out with the butt of his gun. They were lucky. Soasa might have blown them up instead.

Rommond ran, keeping low to the ground, using the wall as cover, and the haze as camouflage. He took his pistol out. It would not do much, but if he was to die this day, he would at least take half a dozen demons with him. In Hell, he would kill some more.

He took out several lone soldiers, pulling them into the dark alleyways, but he stayed near his destroyed landship, periodically surveying the troopers there, who carried Tomdan away. He almost felt like charging after them, but he knew it would be suicide. Part of him almost did not care.

When they were gone, the shell of the Hopebreaker was abandoned. Rommond returned to it and placed his hands upon the hull, and he grimaced from the heat. His head sunk down, and he whispered a lament, a little obituary for the iron dead.

It's just a piece of a metal, a part of him thought.

"No!" he whispered firmly to himself. "It's a symbol."

You broke them, he thought. *You don't need that symbol any more*.

But it was a symbol of many things. He ripped the name plate from the landship and held it up. He was reminded of the one he already had in his quarters, from the landship that Brooklyn took his name. Not his real name, not the one the Ootana tribe gave to him, but it was real to Brooklyn, and that made it real to Rommond too. He patted the buckled hull of the Hopebreaker, reminded that it was the last thing Brooklyn had worked on before his capture, before his death. To Rommond, it was all that was left of him.

Anyone else might have said: *What about the memories?* But as Rommond held up the name plate, he felt a growing anguish, because no matter how strong his love for Brooklyn was, he was finding it hard to remember all the little details that he once cherished.

"I'm starting to forget your face," he whispered, speaking to the metal, to the flames, to the husk and ruin, perhaps even to the fleeting memories themselves.

He heard a footstep behind him, and then a voice. "Perhaps I can remind you."

Chapter Twenty

AN IRON RAIN

The smog filled up the sky, until the spires of buildings could not be seen, until the city itself did not look like a city, but a place where the smoke gathered. It wafted up in plumes, offering the Skyshaker shelter, blinding the Treasury's greedy eyes.

The gunfire stopped, and there was peace in the heavens, even if it might only be a momentary peace, a truce called by man-made weather. Cantro stopped the engines, which clattered noisily until they wound down to no sound at all. The Skyshaker drifted there, letting the gentle winds guide it, letting the air support it.

"How long did you ask for?" Cantro queried when Taberah emerged from the gun turret and returned to the wheel.

"I didn't specify."

Cantro pursed his lips, and Taberah knew that he did not approve.

I don't know how long we'll need, she thought.

Boulder never returned to the cargo bay, where Doctor Mudro toiled endlessly to get his own balloons prepared. The desperate flight of the Skyshaker, the rocking and the dodging, had damaged some of them, and had mixed up others, tangling their wires, which Mudro spent ages trying to unravel.

Then the smog came back, and Mudro knew that he had no more time to prepare. He pulled the lever down on the hatch door and let some of the balloons slip out. They inflated as they went, and the thin cords kept them attached to the vessel, all at varying lengths. He worked until his fingers had blisters, puffing on his pipe between each wave of balloons shoved through the hatch.

It took over an hour to get them all out, by which time Mudro was looking for more leaf to fill up his pipe again.

"We're all set," he called into the intercom.

"Let's hope it works," Taberah replied.

Mudro took a long inhale. He hoped it would not be his last.

The crew of the Skyshaker waited for a long time, knowing that this respite offered them sanctuary, but did nothing for Rommond or the others down below. For now the smog was helping, but if it remained for too long, it would be the end of them all.

Then, as if to answer all those fervent prayers, it began to break. A vicious and cold wind blew from the north, and though the smog gun still spewed its grey venom, the breeze dispersed it, until here and there parts of the Treasury balloons began to appear through the haze.

Yet they were not the only ones, for dozens of

other balloons, bearing the emblem of the Resistance, filled the sky. Though the Treasury still had close to a hundred of its own fleet up there, they knew they were no match for the Skyshaker and its reinforcements, which appeared as if by magic.

And so they fled. The gunners abandoned their posts and helped the other crew guide the balloons far from the city, to the other Treasury refuges. The Treasury was a betting sort, but it did not continue raising the stakes on what it thought to be a losing bet. Money could not be made if they were dead.

"They bought it!" Mudro cried out, and he took a celebratory puff.

"Good work," Taberah replied. "Your decoys look just like the real thing."

"From afar," Mudro said. "Thank the heavens they didn't look at them up close. And thank the heavens the Treasury did not open fire anew. My decoys can't fire back."

To anyone in the city below, it seemed that the Treasury had all but abandoned them, though they still had many coin-counters in the city's banks. The sky was firmly in the control of the Resistance, whose emblems were illuminated by moonlight and gaslight. Regime soldiers far below attempted to shoot them down, but none of them had expected the Resistance to find a way of taking to the sky. That had always been the Treasury's domain, and with the Treasury essentially working for the Regime, or not openly opposing it, few saw a need to develop anti-aircraft guns.

Yet they should have.

The bombs began to fall on Blackout. Cantro drove the Skyshaker over the city, high enough to avoid the sentry gunfire, and low enough to see and strike the landships down below. The airship swept over the roofs of buildings, dropping its deadly ordnance on the barracks and bunkers, on the mounted gun positions and the moving convoys, and on every single target on Rommond's exhaustive list.

Some of the bombs went astray, blowing up buildings, or destroying monuments, though the latter were of the Iron Emperor, who had destroyed the more artistic monuments of the city's older times. Though many of those monstrosities fell, there were always more carvings of that illusive ruler, making his presence felt in places he had never visited.

The bombs fell like the iron tears of gods, who seemed forever weeping. While the smaller gods seemed to shed bullets, the greater gods had now joined in the metal mourning. For every tear dropped, a thousand more would flow from the eyes of the wounded and bereaved in the city far below.

Blackout burned. Fires started in every corner, in every nook, in every metal ruin of a landship. Buildings collapsed and trucks overturned, and many of the Regime soldiers began to abandon their posts and vehicles, dropping their guns and fleeing, or raising their hands, or raising their white flags.

"That's everything on Rommond's list," Alakovi said. Several of her Vixens entered the room; some cheered, while others stood there silently.

"He didn't list the Treasury HQ," Taberah replied.

"Deliberately."

"But they need to be taken out."

"He knows what he's doing, Taberah."

"Well, he's not up here," she replied. "And he's not responding to my calls."

"If you take out their HQ, there'll be no chance of turning them to our side."

"Turning them to our side? Do you hear yourself?"

"They'll join us if we offer the better deal."

"The Regime is still more powerful than us, Alakovi."

"Then why did the Treasury's fleet flee?"

"Because we feigned power."

"Then we can feign some more."

Taberah shook her head. "I think we should take out the Treasury while we still have a chance."

Alakovi grabbed her by the arm. "No, girl. You don't get to make that choice. Only Rommond does. You never learned that lesson, did you?"

"Rommond keeps making mistakes," Taberah replied, reefing her arm from the Matron's grip. "He keeps missing opportunities."

"He made a mistake letting you on board," Alakovi said. "He keeps making that mistake."

"Take it up with him," Taberah barked.

"No," the Matron said. "I'll take it up with you."

More Vixens flooded the room. Soon Taberah found that none of Rommond's other crew were there, not even Cantro. The Vixens stood with arms folded and eyes grim. They blocked every exit.

Chapter Twenty-one

THE GRAND TREASURER

R ommond turned to face a familiar figure. The
sound of a metal cane preceded the man who
held it: Solsan Winceward, the Grand Treasurer. He
wore a velvet black suit, with his coat tails almost
reaching to the ground, and around his neck he wore
a huge golden chain, and on his fingers many large
golden rings. Gold might have been worthless now,
but it reminded everyone of who the real power in
the old world was.

The Grand Treasurer was never seen without his
top hat, which towered above him. The richer the
man, the taller the hat. It was no wonder then that so
many never wore a hat all.

Winceward stopped suddenly and planted his
cane in the ground. It was black with a golden knob
at the top and a golden band at the bottom. It made
a tremendous sound when he walked, and no doubt
this was its intent, for he had no need for a walking
stick at all. He waited for the echo of it to die out
before adjusting his golden spectacles to glare down
pitifully on the poor man before him.

"Rommond," he said, followed by a tut, as if he
had just caught a child stealing from the rich. He held

his thin, curling black moustache between his thumb and index finger, and began to curl it anew, like the minting of a new iron coil.

"Don't pretend you didn't know it was me," the general replied. "Your cane announces your arrival. My bombs do the same."

"And look at the damage you have done," Winceward said, glancing about. "You have cost this city quite a pretty penny, not to mention the loss of lives."

"Do you treasure lives now?"

"We always did, Rommond. That's why we didn't fight the Regime."

"I thought it was because they let you cling to some semblance of power."

"Power is nothing without the people that grant it," Winceward said, "and who will pay their taxes when they are all dead?"

"So they are a means to an end."

"Everything is a means to an end."

"I thought for you money was the means, and the end."

"You always were too smart for your own good. It will be the death of you."

Rommond reached for his gun, but several Treasury snipers shot it from his hand.

"Do try and co-operate, Rommond," Winceward said. "We want that head of yours fully intact."

The Treasury mob swelled. Larger men, with muscles instead of guns, seized Rommond and tied his hands. They dragged him after the Grand Treasurer, who led them into the Treasury headquarters, and into a dimly-lit cellar, the kind of place that Rommond would have conducted an interrogation.

So this is mine, he thought.

"You owe us quite a lot," Winceward said. "All those loans you received. We never saw a penny from them, did we? Not a single coil."

"Yet you still gave them."

"You know quite well that I only approved the first one. There are others in the Treasury that are more generous than I. How foolish of them."

He glanced to his aide, who turned around and ushered in several guards. They pushed and shoved an old lady, who was tied and gagged. It was the Baroness Ebronah, and as she was hounded forward, she tripped and stumbled over her voluminous skirts.

"Some want things to go back to the way things were," Winceward said, gesturing towards Ebronah, who raised her pointed chin to him.

"Surely things were better then," Rommond replied.

"For some, yes," Winceward admitted. "But for me, no. When we were royalty, every city was its own kingdom, and every kingdom had its crown. In the Treasury there is only one crown worth wearing." He tipped his top hat and gave a sickly smile.

"You might benefit now," Rommond said, "but when you stop being useful to the Regime, they will replace you like they are replacing all of us. *Our* civilisation means nothing to them. The Iron Emperor wants racial purity. And you are far from pure."

"Have you even met the Iron Emperor?" Winceward asked.

"No," the general replied. "I don't need to meet the Devil to know I must oppose him."

The Grand Treasurer laughed. "The Devil. What a convenient image you've painted. But he hasn't painted it like that. If you go past the Iron Wall, you'll see. If you go to Ironhold, you'll see. There he is not just a god, he is the only one. What he says, others do. Unquestioning loyalty."

"A cult," Rommond spat.

"And what is the Resistance? Some dare not question the illustrious Rommond."

"I don't lead to death and ruin."

"Are you sure? Look what you've done to this city. You've caused more destruction than the Iron Empire ever did. You're a menace to society, Rommond, a menace. Everywhere you go, things turn to dust. Have you never thought of retiring?"

Rommond smiled. "No."

"That's too bad. I'm afraid we must retire you, put you out to pasture, so to speak. People who don't pay their debts end up paying with the only thing of value they have left: their lives. And with the hefty reward the Iron Emperor has put on your head, I think that is the only way to settle your accounts."

Rommond looked at Ebronah, who continued to aim her pointed chin at Winceward.

"If I must die, then so be it," Rommond said, "but the Baroness has nothing to do with this."

"Don't insult my intellect, Rommond. She might have given you her own money, but that still undermines everything we have done to establish and restore order to this city."

Rommond shook his head. "Ever the politician."

"You should have tried it, Rommond. It suited General Leadman in Copperfort, did it not?"

"He's a traitor."

"He's an opportunist," Winceward said. "A realist, even. You're still living your fantasy, fighting a war you cannot win. You see everything as black and white. For me, there are no enemies. Everyone is a potential ally. Everyone can be a friend of the Treasury."

"So long as they pay."

Winceward's mouth twitched, and his wiry moustache shuddered. "So long as they pay."

They heard a scoff from the Baroness.

"And you," Winceward said, turning to her. He prodded her with his cane. "What have you got to say for yourself?"

She humphed and turned away, which did more to irritate the Grand Treasurer than any verbal response. It seemed that she would not give him the time of day. Rommond hoped that she would not end up giving up her life instead.

Winceward took it out on Rommond, striking him across the face with his cane, knocking one of the general's teeth out. Blood dribbled down Rommond's face, and he breathed heavy, but he would not cry out. He focused his pain in the glare he gave the Grand Treasurer; he transmuted it into hate.

"Will you talk now, Baroness?" Winceward asked. "He's not so pretty without all his teeth, is he? Then again, maybe it reminds you of someone. What was your old husband's name? Rodford? Wasn't he a gentle soul? Too gentle to lead us."

Rommond knew this would upset her. Rodford had served as the first Grand Treasurer after the demons came and ousted the old royalty, after they slayed the ageing kings and queens. He really was a gentle sort. He invoked the ire of his then newly-founded organisation by donating money to the poor. Treasury money. Rich people's money. No wonder they turned on him when the chance came.

"If you think you can hurt me with words," the Baroness said, her voice shaking, "then you are wrong, Winceward. You have *always* been wrong. That is the only reason why you rule the Treasury now, in this wrong era, in this wrong world. Tell me, what is there to buy under the Regime's repressive rules? The Iron Emperor has outlawed anything worth purchasing. Can you hang a painting on your wall if it is not of *him*? Can you buy a sculpture for your courtyard if it is not of *him*? The books burn in towers, and the libraries fill with propaganda. What do you save your money for, Winceward? A rainy day? When will it rain again here? When will it snow? A better tomorrow? We are old, Winceward. There are not many tomorrows left. What of the future? What of it? One day, perhaps one day soon, there will be no future for us. What do we leave behind? Children? No. My children are dead, and what others I would have had, would have been demons, had I not used the amulets. What then? Works? No. There are no more writers or artists in our time. Art is another child of humanity, and it is dead. *He* made sure of that. We leave behind nothing, Winceward, no legacy. You are not quite as old as I, but if you get to my age, you will not be counting coils; you will be counting regrets. By then it will be too late. What fortune you have built will be spent by others' hands. Truly, it will only be spent by *his* hands, that demon king in the east, who made us all turn in our gold for iron."

To Rommond's surprise, Winceward was silent throughout this speech, and it seemed to move him, as it did the general, as it did many of the other Treasurers and guards inside the room. It seemed that they were still human after all.

But there was still money to be made. The price was Rommond's head.

Chapter Twenty-two

A DEBT TO BE PAID

R ommond was brought to the guillotine, which was already red with the blood of others, of so-called traitors. Ebronah's husband had been one of them, yet he had always been loyal to the people, loyal to the poor.

"How fitting," Winceward said, as Rommond was strapped in place, "that you should lose your head. Is that not what happened to Brooklyn also?"

Rommond growled and struggled in his bonds.

"You know," the Grand Treasurer continued, "I would have thought they'd have wanted you intact, that they might have paid more for the whole body. But you really angered them. Your head on a pike is all they want. That is one work of art they will proudly present to the world. You never know, Rommond. You might even feature in a museum one day."

Rommond could only see Winceward's shiny black boots, with the strip of gold around the heel. He could barely twist his head to see Ebronah there, who tried not to look. He wanted to say his last goodbyes. He had not seen her in years. What a sorry reunion it had been.

"Let me take his place," she volunteered, though

her voice wavered.

"No," the general said. "This is my debt to pay."

"You can borrow it from me," she said.

"I've already borrowed enough."

"For once," Winceward said, "I agree with Rommond. His borrowing days are over. Indeed, for these last few years, he has been living on borrowed time. You might have a hefty fortune, Baroness, but your life is not worth more than Rommond's head. What you made in eighty years, we will make tenfold in eighty seconds."

The guillotine blade was pulled into place. Rommond heard it shake in its frame. He shook in sympathy with it. Ebronah shook in sympathy with him. The Grand Treasurer felt no sympathy at all. In his eyes there were no tears, only lust and greed.

"It's nothing personal, Rommond," Winceward said. "Business is business."

How Rommond had heard those lines before, from the mouths of those trying to kill him. It was personal to him. It was personal to the Iron Emperor.

The seconds counted down, and Rommond gulped hard. In moments he would not get to gulp again. He thought about his life. Forty-two years. He had lived a good one, even if those last few years were marred by pain. Now it would all be over. He could see Brooklyn once again.

There was a click, and then an explosion rocked the room, which quickly filled with smoke. Shouts followed, and people lashed out blindly at their assailants. By the time the smoke cleared, the Treasury's guards were knocked out on the ground, and Rommond had been freed from the guillotine.

Then it became clear who had rescued them: the Regime. Rommond shook his head in disbelief as he saw the dozen troops, rallying behind an officer. A familiar officer: Jacob.

"That's him!" Jacob shouted. "That's Rommond, the Resistance leader!"

"What the hell are you doing?" the Grand Treasurer asked.

"We received intel that you are smuggling that traitor out of the city."

"Does it look like it?"

"It looks like you've arranged the assassination of our informant," Jacob said, pointing to Ebronah. "The Baroness has always been a spy for the ... Iron Empire." Rommond could tell that Jacob had almost said *Regime*. He had to be careful. He had to wear the uniform on his tongue as well.

"This is madness!" Winceward bawled. "I've received commands straight from the Iron Emperor himself. We were just about to behead the general."

"Save it for the courts," Jacob said. "The day we trust Treasury scum is the day the Iron Emperor falls. Long live the Iron Emperor."

This was followed by a series of hails from the guards, and a very half-hearted hail from Whistler. Soasa gave none at all.

The Regime troops hauled the Grand Treasurer out into the corridor, rumpling his suit, which cost more than the clothes of everyone else then present. Winceward waved his cane in protest, yelling taunts and threats, which did not cost a thing.

"Keep an eye on him," Jacob said. "We'll look after Rommond."

The soldiers gave a firm salute, then turned their backs on their commander. At that point Soasa ignited a stick of dynamite, cast it into the corridor, and slammed the door shut. They heard a series of shouts and cries, followed by an immense explosion, which shook the chamber. Those soldiers would not turn their backs again.

Jacob untied Rommond, while Whistler untied Ebronah, before recoiling as she tried to greet him with a kiss.

"Did you miss me?" Jacob asked the general.

"You're full of surprises," Rommond said, rubbing his wrists.

"The good kind," Whistler added with a smile. Jacob grinned at him.

"Yes, the good kind," the general said, shaking his head in disbelief. He was certain he was done for. He almost did not mind. "How did you even know I was here?"

Jacob shrugged. "We asked around."

"You *asked*?"

"You'd be surprised how well that works ... when in uniform."

"And if that doesn't work," Soasa said, "I can ask *my* way."

"I see I sent the right team," Rommond acknowledged. "A smuggler, a saboteur, and a spy. A perfect trio." He ruffled Whistler's hair. The general was so happy, and so relieved, Jacob almost expected him to ruffle his hair too.

But there was no time to celebrate. There was still much work to be done. Rommond brought Ebronah aside.

"With Winceward dead," he said, "who will take his place?"

"That will go up for a vote."

"So it isn't about blood?"

She cupped his face, as she might have done so many times with her husband. "We're only royalty in memory now, sweetheart."

He held her hands, bringing them together almost like a sign of prayer. "Can you win that vote?"

"I never thought about it."

"Then think about it now," Rommond said. "You've always been one of our strongest supporters. Think of what you could do as Grand Treasurer."

They called a council immediately, and the rich and powerful used their secret routes to enter the Treasury Chambers, which were as ornate as anyone would expect them to be. The ceiling was twenty feet high, with immense chandeliers made of glass hanging from it, and floral carvings and designs made into the coving. Tapestries hung from the walls, and huge red curtains stood like sentinels on either side of the colossal windows, which were so finely made that they had largely withstood the assault on the city. The room was so ornate it was essentially a work of art. It was a surprise that the Regime had let it stand at all.

"The tide is turning," Ebronah announced to the well-dressed crowd, many of whom judged her with their spectacles or monocles. "If the Treasury is about opportunity, then we *cannot* ignore this one. With proper funding, the Resistance can win this war, and we no longer need to serve as puppets to the real power of the Iron Empire. We can restore things to the way they were."

There was discussion in the crowd, with some approving nods, and some disapproving glares. They seemed evenly divided. Some reminisced about the past, while others spoke of stability, which was not something the Resistance seemed to offer. Others said they had already supported the Resistance in the past, and Blackout had fallen to the Regime anyway.

A vote was called for the new Grand Treasurer, with Winceward's chosen successor, Ferdinand Hullsburg, seen by many as the favourite, despite him not even being in the city at the time. Hullsburg was not quite as ruthless as Winceward was, but he shared many of his policies and views, including the policy of acquiescence and collaboration with the Regime, a viewpoint the Baroness made very clear had brought them all to their present ruin.

The Counter began his careful task, checking and rechecking the votes, which were supposed to be made anonymously, but with so many of the Treasurers openly sharing their views, some supporting or condemning Ebronah and the Resistance, it was largely clear where everybody stood.

The Counter called Ebronah to his table, to share the preliminary result. She sunk her head at the news, and the general approached her.

"How many more votes do you need?" he asked.

"Two," Ebronah said.

Rommond swiftly unleashed his pistol and shot two of the opposing Treasurers between the eyes.

"How many now?"

"It's a tie."

Rommond pointed his gun at the others who opposed Ebronah's election. "Is it?" he asked. "Or did you all accidentally vote for the wrong person?"

Several of the Treasurers immediately switched sides, casting their ballots in favour of Ebronah, coming up with all manner of excuses for why they had voted erroneously the first time around.

"This is most unorthodox," the Counter complained.

"You learned to adapt when the demons came," Rommond said. "Learn to adapt now, or you'll meet new demons when I send you all to Hell."

The Counter began re-counting reluctantly, and sure enough, Ebronah won the vote. Her true supporters cheered, while the turncoats reluctantly clapped, likely celebrating more their own survival than the Baroness' victory. They might have lost the vote, but they lived to make a profit another day, and for many of them, that was all that truly mattered.

Chapter Twenty-three

GRUDGE

On board the Skyshaker, Taberah turned to face her accusers. She rested against the controls, and returned their glare with her own.

"This is a bad time," she said.

"It's the perfect time," Alakovi replied.

"What do you want?"

"I want you off this ship."

"You'll have to throw me off."

"We finally agree on something then," the Matron said.

Taberah reached for a rifle beneath the control panel, but the Copper Matron raised a rifle of her own. "Ah ah, there's no point tryin' to grab for that."

"Rommond won't forgive you for this," Taberah said.

"He forgave *you*, and you never had his interests in mind."

Taberah scoffed. "And you do?"

"Always. He's like a son to me."

Taberah pointed to herself, to her heart. "He's like a brother to me."

The Copper Matron's glower was unyielding. "One you stabbed in the back, one you couldn't help but be envious of."

"I didn't envy him," Taberah said.

"Only his position, his power."

"One day you'll have to let that go, like Rommond did."

"No," the Matron said. "I have to let *you* go."

"So you're going to kill me then," Taberah said. "And my child."

"With you as its mother, Taberah, that child might as well be already dead."

Taberah bit her lip and turned her gaze away. She saw the line of Copper Vixens blocking every exit, blocking her escape. She could never fight them all.

"So, this is it," Taberah said, holding up her hands.

"This is it," Alakovi said, stepping forward.

"I'm supposed to just give in? I'm supposed to just give up?"

"Yes, you're supposed to do those things."

"I'm supposed to not resist, not fight, not flee, not run?"

The Copper Matron nodded. "Yes."

"Then what makes you better than the Regime?"

Alakovi grumbled and ground her teeth together, as if they were feasting on Taberah's bones.

"You think you have Rommond's best interests in mind," Taberah said, "but you don't. You don't understand him. You never did, and you never will. He sees the bigger picture. *I* see the bigger picture. And right now that bigger picture is outside these windows. It's happening on the ground below." She pointed at the windscreen, from where they could see the city burning. She hoped that Rommond was not burning too.

Alakovi shook her head violently. She almost seemed on the verge of thumping her chest, and of thumping Taberah soon after. "You," she said, pointing an accusatory finger, "are a manipulator, and you're even doin' it now, tryin' to distract me, tryin' to make the call for the good fight. Well, this is the good fight, gettin' rid of you. We're stronger without you."

"No," Taberah said. "No, you're not. And what you're doing now shows just how weak you are."

Alakovi stormed forward and smacked Taberah across the face, knocking her into the control panels. Taberah turned back to her, her cheek as red as her flaming hair, and her eyes more fiery still.

"Beat me if you want," she said. "You'll never break me."

"I'll kill you," Alakovi threatened.

"And you'll *still* never break me."

"It doesn't matter," the Matron said. "So long as you're not there to break Rommond any more."

She clicked her fingers, and several of the Copper Vixens strolled up, with smugness in their strides. Taberah knew many of them. At one point, they had been her sisters too. They had exchanged the secret grips and words, and they had shared so much in their sorority. Now she was outside the pale of their group, and it felt like she was outside the pale of all humanity.

Some of the women grabbed her harshly, while others, those who were closer to her in those bygone days, held her more gently. Some exchanged sympathetic glances, but most greeted her with glares, if they even looked at her at all. They led her away from the controls, which Cantro took back over, and led her down to a lower deck, where many others of the Resistance turned a blind eye to what was happening. Those among the Order who could see were not there to do it.

So many thoughts flashed in Taberah's mind. She wondered how she would die, if they would shoot her, or, more likely, throw her from the airship, like a pirate forced to walk the plank. Perhaps in the chaos in Blackout far below they would not find her body, or maybe it would be showcased by the Regime, proof of what happens to those who defy them. She thought of her child, and tried hard not to. What a terrible life the baby would be born into, and yet it was better than not being born at all. She thought of Brogan and what a terrible life he had lived so far, and wondered if he wished she had not brought him into this dying world. She wished she could say she loved him. She wished she could say goodbye.

Her thoughts consumed her, so much so that she barely noticed the cramps in her stomach, which seized her as much as the hands of the Copper Vixens. But they grew in intensity, until she could not think of anything else. As they led her down a corridor, Taberah suddenly stopped and grabbed the wall. She doubled over, clutching her stomach, and she cried out from the pain.

"Don't you be tryin' that with me," Alakovi said. "I don't fall for your tricks like the others do. You can't use your woman's guile on me. I've got me own."

But Taberah's cries did not abate—they increased.

The pain ripped through her, and she found it difficult to stand. Then all eyes looked to the floor beneath her feet, where there was a growing pool of blood.

Chapter Twenty-four

SHAKEN

Blackout was mostly under Resistance control, but aboard the Skyshaker there was a frenzy, as if a new battle had just started. Taberah was rushed to Doctor Mudro, whom the Copper Vixens had kept locked in the cargo hold, but by that time there was little he could do. He got the baby out, but it was dead.

Alakovi's grudge was spent. Though she had intended to send Taberah away, or maybe even kill her, this was punishment enough. She was the Copper Matron. She knew what it was like to lose a child. Anyone who conspired with her against the unpopular Taberah now felt a looming guilt, strong enough to match Taberah's looming grief.

The news spread to the city below, but Rommond's lieutenants made a conspiracy of their own: they told each other, and anyone else who knew, Jacob included, to keep it from him. The last thing he needed was to hear such terrible news, and know his own crew might have had a part in it. People looked to him for guidance. Now the entire city of Blackout looked to him too. So many had been shaken. He could not be one of them.

Jacob managed to slip away and return to the Skyshaker in a basket lowered down on an immense rope, like a gigantic umbilical cord, hauling him back into the womb of the airship. The mood there was grim. Few would have thought that they had just won back their capital. There were no celebrations, just silence.

Mudro led Jacob to Taberah's room.

"She's alone," he said.

Those words never had so much meaning, so much power, so much sting.

Jacob entered the room slowly. It was dark, darker than it needed to be. There were gas lamps and candles there, but they were all snuffed out. The shadows crowded around Taberah's bed like mourners. She sat up, holding the sheets. She had nothing else to hold.

"Are you okay?" Jacob asked.

She did not respond. What tears she had shed, what screams she had made, were overwhelmed by silence. The room was thick with it, as if before Jacob had entered, there was silence enough for two.

Taberah did not look at him. She kept her gaze upon the farthest wall, where perhaps she saw something that he did not. The shadows did not gather there. They kept close to her, where they could hide her eyes, those fiery eyes, doused like the nearby lamps.

Jacob stepped further into the room, his head slumped low. His feet barely made any noise upon the ground. He was used to sneaking. He was not used to this.

He sat down on one of the chairs positioned

around the bed. In a few months time, they might have been sat upon by joyous people, celebrating the birth of a new child. He would have been one of them, perhaps the most joyous of them all. Now he had the same seat, but nothing of the joy. What sorrow he felt, giving birth deep inside his soul, he knew was but a fraction of what Taberah must be feeling, if she felt anything at all.

What can I say? he thought, and he thought of nothing, so he let silence speak for him. Even the silence was full of apologies, full of remorse, of regret.

An hour passed without a word, without a stir, without a baby's coo or cry, and though it was only an hour, it felt like a lifetime—like the lifetime that little unborn child never got to live.

In time Jacob felt that there was nothing he could do there. He felt like he was somehow intruding on her silent communication with something else. He felt he was an imposter in his false uniform, pretending to be a soldier, an officer, pretending to be a father. He knew for certain he was not a husband, not a lover. He was not sure he was anything at all.

He stood up slowly and made his way towards the door.

"Jacob," she called. Her voice was weak. She had lost a lot of blood. She had lost a lot of strength. Jacob hoped that she had not lost the will to live.

He turned back to her. The shadows shifted on her face. For the first time, he could see the glisten in her eyes. He could see the pain.

"It was going to be a girl," she said. "It was going to be ... she was going to be ..." She trailed off, but

Jacob stayed there, because he knew she had more to say. "I lost my first," she said. "I was seven months in. Mudro told me it was a girl, but I could already tell. Elizah. That was going to be … that was her name. God's promise. That's what it means. She was God's promise to me. He promised me a child."

Jacob stood there in silence, soaking in her sorrow.

"It was the Harvest," Taberah continued. "I lost her because of the Harvest. I saw the desert in my dreams. I didn't know that it also meant my womb. And I chased her. I chased her ghost. I thought … there had to be a way. It wasn't natural how I lost her. There had to be something supernatural to bring her back. But I never found her. Well…"

She held back whatever it was she was going to say, and she dug her nails into the blanket, as if she was trying desperately not to let it go.

"But I thought," she continued, "after all these years, everything I did back then, things I'm not proud of, but things I would do again, had somehow worked. I felt her. Inside of me. It was her. I could tell. A mother can tell, Jacob. A mother can tell. It *was* Elizah. She came back to me."

She finally let go of the blanket. It slumped to the floor, lifeless.

"And now she's gone again."

"You still have Whistler," Jacob said, and he said it as softly as he could. "You still have me."

He knew it was not enough, but he also knew that, for the time being, perhaps for all the time she had left, it would have to be.

* * *

Jacob left that dark, depressing room, and he found that outside was a little darker than it had been before, and a little bit more depressing. He found Mudro there, resting against the wall, soothing his sorrows with the smoke of the leaf.

"I wish I was a better medic," Mudro pined.

"What about a better magician?"

Mudro smothered his sigh by placing his pipe in his mouth. "I can do many tricks, but I can't put the rabbit back in the hat."

"This isn't the first time," Jacob said.

"She told you?"

"Yeah."

"I bet she didn't tell you everything."

"I'm not sure I want to know more," Jacob said. "At least it means she got over it once before, so she can get over it again."

"You don't know what she was like back then," the doctor replied, and for a moment he held his pipe away, and leaned in close. "Whatever sicknesses there are of the body, there are also some of the brain. She obsessed over that child. That's how I met her." He sighed. "The things she had us do, the unnatural things we tried. She chased ghosts before she ever chased demons. It was one obsession, one single-mindedness, that transferred to another."

Jacob shuddered. "Maybe she can turn that on the Regime," he suggested. "Maybe she can obsess about killing them."

"Oh, she will, I'm sure. And the sooner she does,

the better. We used every trick we had to get this city back, and one of those was the radios. You can bet your life that we weren't the only ones listening. I hate to say it, Jacob, but Taberah doesn't have time to mope around. She doesn't have time to stay in bed. I called in my dummy cavalry to help us clear the skies, but you can be sure that the Regime's cavalry is very real."

"I'm not sure she's ready for that," Jacob said. "It's too soon."

"They won't care. For them, the sooner the better."

"I … I'm not sure I can go in and tell her to snap out of it."

"Neither am I, and I'm not even sure she'd listen. She never listened when she was chasing illusions. I just wonder if the things she was chasing were really in her own head."

"We all have our ghosts and demons," Jacob said.

Mudro raised an eyebrow, and let out a long puff of smoke, like a spectre. "We sure do."

Chapter Twenty-five

FORTIFYING

Jacob returned to the city streets, where Rommond was leading the preparations. The city was half in ruins, but the general knew well that what was coming from the east would level the other half, and bury all of them with it.

The city was fortified as best as possible. Fires were put out, doors were repaired, and makeshift barricades were put in place. Yet few thought that this would make any difference, and many cast a distrustful eye at Rommond, who had for so long been the boogeyman whose face lined their streets.

The Baroness tried to call back the Treasury balloons that had fled the city, only this time to defend it against a greater enemy: the Regime's most elite troops, the Iron Guard. Yet those balloons were far from the city by now, and would take time to return, and some of the Treasurers were not entirely keen to return at all. Switching sides was a costly move. It had already cost them enough.

Jacob found Rommond sitting down with Soasa and Whistler around a fire. The night had thickened. Few expected to get any sleep at all. Those who did might never wake again.

"Everyone's on edge," Jacob said.

"Better to be on edge than think you can't be pushed over it," Rommond replied.

"They're really coming?"

"Oh, trust me, Jacob. They're coming."

"I kind of feel like saying, let's quit while we're ahead."

"We can quit the city, but there's only one way to quit life. Those machine men will be happy to help you."

"You've fought them before?"

"Only once."

"What happened?"

"I lost my biggest gun to them."

"The Iron Wall?"

Rommond nodded. "We didn't call it that, but it was a wall all the same. It's what stopped the demons' advance for so long. We had the technological edge. But you see, we stopped with machinery. Their scientists, if we can call them that, they went too far. Brooklyn predicted this. He said the iron spirits were restless. He said they spoke of abominations."

"You know, I'm not feeling very enthusiastic right now."

"This isn't a morale speech," Rommond said.

"So the gun didn't work on them?" Whistler asked, hugging his legs.

"It worked just fine, but when it knocked out a regiment, the others didn't break. We could always count on the railway gun to make the enemy quake, make them quiver. But these weren't men. God, they weren't even demons. They were bits of men, bits of demon, but they were mostly machine. You fire a bullet at a landship; it doesn't flinch. And you bet your ass it has a bigger gun."

"Maybe I won't bet my ass then," Jacob mused.

"So when do we get the morale speech?" Whistler asked.

Rommond forced a smile. "I'm not sure there is one, Brogan." He paused for a moment and then took out his revolver with its diamond-tipped bullets. "Well, maybe this is all the morale we need."

"I hope you've got one of those for all of us," Jacob said.

"It depends who 'us' is," the general replied. "I've got Alakovi sending down crates right now. She's been working on them since I perfected the design."

"I hope she had less trouble with them than you had."

"So do I, Jacob. And I hope they work."

"You mean you haven't tested them?"

"I've tested them on metal, on armour plating, on a salvaged piece of the Lifemaker's hull, which is about as thick as you can get. They work on those. But on machine men? Who knows?"

Jacob shuddered. "I guess we won't have long to find out."

"We either learn that these guns really work, or we die."

"I guess we won't be disappointed for long then. Unless, you know, there really is a Hell."

"Oh, there is, Jacob," Rommond said, and he span the barrel of his revolver, like the spinning doors of life and death. "We're already there."

Chapter Twenty-six

THE BATTLE OF
THE BLACK BARGE

The wait was nerve-wrecking. Some fled the city of Blackout, but others locked themselves in their homes. Rommond's depleted army had nowhere to run to, and no where to hide. Most of them hovered above the city in the Skyshaker, with no one daring to sleep, lest they find themselves waking in a nightmare. Rommond and his trio of smugglers stayed in the city below, where they converted the remaining smog guns into an anti-airship battery.

It was dawn before the Iron Guard reached the city, and the sun was hesitant to rise. The mechanical men travelled in an immense airship known only as the Black Barge, for it was a huge flattened rectangular vessel, featureless, like so many of the Regime's creations. This was not art; it was brute force.

The airship glided slowly towards them, less like a vessel of war and more like a barge of the dead. At times pale green lights flickered, like the deathly version of the living's candle flames, and many who saw them feared that they would board the ship and add a new pale flicker of their own.

The Iron Guard were the Regime's most elite

force, a mixture of man and machine, the personal guard of the Iron Emperor himself. They were rarely seen away from his palace in Ironhold, and when they were, it showed that the Emperor had taken a personal interest—even a personal offence—in the Resistance's advancements.

The barge drifted towards them, barely standing out against the bleak sky, which might have tried to hide itself in clouds, so as not to be seen by those watchful mechanical eyes. It was not clear how it supported itself, how it floated, how it rose, fell, turned or drifted. Anything that might have shown this was hidden in the immense rectangular hull. There was no discernible movement of crew, and no noise. It sailed the sky in silence, which made it that much more imposing.

"If it's a ghost ship," Jacob said, "then let us show some ghosts another way to die."

"In faraway lands, they speak of a second death," Rommond mused with a hint of dread. "But it is not ghosts that will haunt us this day. It will be the remnants of men, good men, and the shells of demons, foul demons, forged with our abandoned and broken technology, merged with cogs and welded with wires, running not on blood, but on steam. They do not tire like men. They do not *die* like men. We need to break them like machines."

A siren rung in the Skyshaker, and everyone raced to their posts. A few had managed to doze off, but no one was rested. The crew charged up and down the corridors. And then the door of Taberah's room opened, and she stepped out. A few people paused when they saw her, but duty propelled them on. Her face was grim, almost as grim as that of the Iron Guard themselves. She marched through the airship and took her familiar place at the frontal gun. She was not in the mood to wait around, to do nothing. She was in the mood to kill.

"All set?" Rommond asked over the radio.

"All set," she said, her voice strained, yet the general barely noticed. He still had not been informed of what happened, of her condition, of the actions of the Copper Vixens. She did not tell him. She knew that it was better that way.

All of the gun positions were manned, but the ammunition supplies were very low. They had to win this battle quick, or they would not win it at all. The decoy balloons were released into the wild, for they posed no threat to the Iron Guard. They did not care how many they were facing. Their target would still be the Skyshaker, which they would not merely shake, but would destroy.

The Black Barge sailed above the city. If it had not been made of iron, it would still have been black, for the soot fell upon its frame in thick layers, and though it pumped smoke into the heavens, it pumped soot upon the land below, leaving a dark trail on the red sands, and turning the city's streets from grey to black.

Then the battle began. The Skyshaker dived towards the Black Barge in crusader mode, and Taberah unleashed a hail of gunfire. The bullets bashed off the hull, some bouncing, some buckling, and one or two making tiny punctures, but not enough to cause any real damage. Cantro turned the ship sharply, almost grazing the surface of the Black Barge, and then the Iron Guard answered, with hatches opening and turrets emerging, giving the vessel its much-needed features, but the kind of features that the Resistance did not want it to have. The bullets streamed after the Skyshaker, less chaotically than the Treasury's gunfire was, which made it difficult for Cantro to evade. Yet he evaded most of them, and the crew fired back with a frenzy, and Alakovi sent missiles, which rocked the Black Barge, but did not down it.

On the ground, Rommond manned one of the newly-converted anti-airship guns, while Soasa took the second, and Jacob and Whistler took the third. They were spread out over the city, but the Black Barge was so large that it was in the sight of all. They fired at it, striking it with force, but still it seemed immovable; still it seemed like it could not be taken down at all.

The battle raged like this for half an hour, with neither side seeming to get anywhere, a stalemate of the skies. Yet the Iron Guard had not depleted its ammunition in a recent battle. They could afford to wait it out. The Resistance could not.

Then Rommond saw dark shapes approaching the city from the south, their silhouettes standing out against the emerging sun. They flew fast in the sky.

We have no allies, Rommond thought. That only meant one thing. *They must be enemies.*

And so they were, for in time it was clear that it was El Abra and his pirates, darting towards the city with haste—there to pillage and steal, to take what they could as the two opposing forces were engaged.

"Damn it!" Rommond cried. "As if we need another enemy."

Rommond turned his gun towards them, and prepared to fire. But something told him to wait.

The Red Serpent and its supporting galleons flew straight past the Skyshaker, without a single bullet fired, and then they turned their cannons on the Black Barge. They broke formation, giving the Iron Guard more than one thing to focus on, splitting its fire. They weaved and dodged, showing as much aerial acrobatic skill as Cantro himself.

Rommond was in shock. What made the pirates join the battle was anyone's guess. The general guessed that it was Jacob, that El Abra's reminder of their childhood past had softened him a little, or hardened him against a common foe. Rommond was surprised that El Abra was even still alive, but with his spyglass he could see the pirate prancing above deck, yet prancing less lithely than before, for he was bandaged up around the waist.

The Black Barge had guns enough for all of its assailants, however, and it fired them all in unison. What a terrifying thing it was to hear those guns roar as one, for the boom rocked the sky like thunder. It caught one of El Abra's galleons, which plunged to the ground in flames, but still the others fought on.

What Cantro, Taberah and the rest of the crew had faced against the Treasury now seemed like child's play. They had fought an enemy of numbers, but now they fought just a single target, and they knew what the Treasury felt when it went up against the Skyshaker, but they knew it with an even greater fear.

Bullets tore through the hull of the Skyshaker, piercing the envelope, bursting some of the balloons inside. Boulder was not there to patch them up, and though the Copper Vixens raced to plug those holes, the airship was already losing height, and Cantro struggled with the wheel.

In time the remaining galleons were downed, and El Abra's ship, the Red Serpent, was the only pirate vessel left in flight, joining the Skyshaker in a two-pronged attack. But the Black Barge fired in every direction. It was the Behemoth of the sky, casting jets of flame from both sides, which illuminated the heavens in a terrifying display. No wonder the people of Blackout pledged allegiance to the Iron Emperor. If that devil was over anyone else's city, they would too.

But the battle was getting the Resistance nowhere. What little damage they had done to the Black Barge was magnified on the Red Serpent and the Skyshaker, the former ignited in flame, and the latter struggling to stay afloat. It seemed that both of them would sink to join the galleons that had crashed into the buildings far below.

Then El Abra made his most daring move yet. He climbed up onto the burning deck, and gave a twirl and a kiss to anyone who would see. Then he turned the gigantic wheel, and steered his ship straight into the side of the Black Barge. There it burned anew, but the fire spread, and the Barge itself was ignited. Explosions rocked the hull, and guns and mechanical men were thrown out from the sides.

Then the vessel's nose dipped, and it hurtled down into the city. It struck the old library, and it took out several fortifications, even the Treasury's clock tower. It continued through several streets, tearing down buildings in its way, until it finally halted just before the Treasury's own headquarters, as if to announce, in the most costly manner possible, *We have arrived!*

Chapter Twenty-seven

THE MECHANICAL MEN

The Skyshaker fell slowly into Blackout's streets, landing on top of one of the city's oldest hotels, its remaining buoyancy keeping it from crushing the building. The surviving crew raced outside, clambering onto the roof, climbing down ropes.

Rommond abandoned his anti-airship gun and raced towards the Skyshaker, which was visible from almost any street.

"We need to ground this ship," he called up to his crew, who struggled on the rooftop. "Pull it down, soldiers. Pull it down!"

And they pulled, but it would barely budge. If the Skyshaker could no longer fly, could barely float, it could not truly fight. The battle of the sky was over. The ground had still to be won.

Rommond kicked down the hotel door and raced past many patrons, who shrieked and cowered. He took the stairs several steps at a time, until he emerged on the roof, where the tiles glimmered as the sun dared to rise a little higher in the sky.

"How many landships do we have left?" he asked Alakovi.

"Four," she said.

"Is that all?"

"That's all that are functioning. We had to take some parts to repair the ship."

"Then that'll have to do," the general grumbled.

As they struggled with the Skyshaker, and the wind that tried to seize it, they saw the city burn where the Black Barge had crashed. And in those fires they saw emerging shapes, little black silhouettes that were not so little when viewed up close. Figures that could withstand fire, that could withstand gunfire, that could perhaps withstand death itself.

"The Iron Guard," Rommond whispered, as if even he feared to say their name, to summon them from that realm of nightmare from which they had come. The Black Barge became a barracks, from which issued the Iron Emperor's most terrible and elite soldiers.

"We've no more time for this," the general said, before climbing inside the Skyshaker, and then driving through the hull in one of the remaining landships. He drove over the roof, pulling up tiles, and dived to the ground, falling three stories, and severely denting the front of the vehicle. He was lucky it did not explode. He had attached two ropes to the rear, which pulled the airship with it as he drove, and helped dislodge it from the old hotel.

The crew pulled it down more easily, and Alakovi abandoned her engineering duty to drive one of the other landships. Cantro took the second. Jacob took the third. Rommond cut the ropes tying the airship to his vehicle, and he turned to his remaining soldiers.

"The Skyshaker's still a vessel to reckon with," he

said. "It may not fly, but by God will it fire. We'll lure those machine monsters here, and you better have the airship's guns primed and ready. They'll have theirs."

He did not wait for a response. He dived back inside, taking a gunner with him, and drove straight for the bonfire that consumed the centre of the city. The other landships followed, and the battle for Blackout continued.

Jacob was not keen to be back inside the metal box of a landship, that claustrophobic vessel, that roving coffin. It was dark inside, but the sunlight pierced the city's smog, and so he could easily see where Rommond roamed. Not that it was necessary. The target was pretty obvious. The target of the Iron Guard was pretty obvious too; it was everybody else.

The streets were eerily silent. Few dared take on this mythic foe. They cowered in their houses. Perhaps those who opposed the Resistance hoped that the Iron Guard would liberate the city, restore some order, and then the people could emerge again without fear. But from what Rommond had told him, Jacob knew that the Iron Guard were indiscriminate. If they had been sent to Blackout, it was not to liberate; it was to annihilate.

"What a mess we're in," Jacob said to the gunner who had joined him.

She did not reply. He did not even know her name. She kept her focus on the gun, on the enemy. The silence got to Jacob. He needed something to distract him from his thoughts, from his mounting fears. A little joke might have meant nothing to some, but it meant everything to him.

Then he saw the mechanical men for the first time. They had a human shape, but it was augmented with machinery, with cogs and pistons, with pumps and pulleys, with wires and tubes. Natural anatomy was replicated and replaced with an artificial equivalent, and so the creatures were "enhanced." The humanity was drained from them, and all that was left was a cold-hearted killer, with guns for arms, and a crosshair for eyes.

Jacob shuddered as he saw them, but his gunner did not shudder; she rattled off her gunfire, which knocked down some of the iron monsters, but did not appear to kill them. Jacob felt the gun that Rommond had given him resting in its holster on his belt, augmented with its own machinery. He could not use it from here, and he did not have many diamond-coated bullets to use.

So he drove into the mechanical men, knocking them down, crushing them beneath the heavy treads of the landship. Yet still they seemed to survive all this, and many sat or stood up and began to repair what damage had been caused. Others fired at the four landships, which whizzed through the streets, drawing the attention of the hundreds of machine men who emerged from the Black Barge.

Rommond drew much of their gunfire. It seemed they somehow knew which of the landships he was in. Perhaps it was how he drove, or the tactics he used to weave in and out of them, inviting them to fire on their fellow men, to kill their own as they tried desperately to kill him. He could not turn as sharply in the Menacer Mark II landship as he could in the Hopebreaker, and the hull was not as thick, so it was soon riddled with bullet holes, which were clearly visible to the drivers of the other vehicles.

Rommond led them back towards the Skyshaker, luring out the machine men, who marched in mechanical rhythm, with the percussion of gunfire enhancing their methodical beats. When they approached the Skyshaker, Taberah was ready for them. She still sat in her glass bubble, but she looked as grim and determined as ever, and her fingers were itching on the triggers. Dozens of the enemy were gunned down, but they did not yet die. They struggled on the ground, with parts blown away, with wires disconnected, with their steam pumps no longer generating any steam. The Copper Vixens raced over to the wounded and aimed the guns that Rommond had designed, and put those poor creatures, or those poor machines, out of their mechanical misery.

The first wave had been defeated, and the landship drivers regrouped beside the Skyshaker, where they witnessed the pile of bodies, and the pile of parts, that they had left in their wake. Jacob popped his head outside and wiped his brow; the heat inside was killing him, but it was better than what the Iron Guard would do.

The Resistance savoured this moment of reprieve, this temporary delay of their iron punishment, but their rest was brief. A second and a third flood of figures emerged from the Black Barge, much larger than the first.

"They've brought more men!" Alakovi shouted.

"So be it," Rommond said. "When you bring more wood, you make a bigger fire."

But his confidence was overstated, for that bigger fire was quickly spreading, and it darted towards the Skyshaker in such numbers that the airship would quickly be overwhelmed. So the general led many of the mechanical men away farther into the city, and the drivers of the other landships did the same. All four split up, which forced their assailants to split up too. Some still went for the Skyshaker, but in smaller numbers, and yet Taberah and the remaining crew there still struggled against them.

Jacob found that he was less luring them away and more fleeing from them. Some of them simply walked, but others ran, and their speed was enhanced by piston-powered legs. Trails of smoke and steam were left in their wake, and some of them turned to look in dark alleys not illuminated by the sun, and these were then lit up by gaslit torches on their shoulders, or, in one or two cases, in their eyes.

The landship needed constant attention just to keep it moving. Jacob shovelled coal with one hand and steered with the other. His feet worked the pedals frantically, while his gunner worked the sponson guns, switching back and forth between the right and left, slowing the pursuing enemy.

Then one of the mechanical men caught up, and it jumped on top of the roof of the landship and used the automatic saw it had for a hand to tear straight through the hull. Jacob ducked inside, and in that moment when he took his eyes off the road, he crashed into the side of a building, throwing the Iron

Guard into the rubble. The landship was of little use now, but the gunner stayed inside, arming the guns. Jacob pushed open the hatch and climbed outside, and he grabbed his augmented gun just in time before the machine man broke free of the debris that pinned it in place. A single bullet, a diamond bullet, ended its life, if it had life, but Jacob could already hear the sound of more approaching.

"Come on!" he cried to the gunner, banging the chassis of the landship, but she ignored him. Perhaps she felt safer inside, but Jacob disagreed. That ruined vehicle was a beacon, and its hull offered no protection against the many contraptions that had been surgically attached to those mechanised beasts.

Jacob ran into the city streets, ducking low, searching for shadows to hide in, but finding that the sunlight was searching him out as much as the machine men were, like a spotlight from the sky. He stumbled upon an Iron Guard in his flight, and he missed the mark when he fired at first, but knocked it dead on the second try. He was running out of bullets now. He could not afford to miss again.

At last he found a crack in the side of an abandoned building. He squeezed through, and found the darkness comforting. Perhaps this was a Hope-house, a haven for the city's many drug addicts. Now it was his haven, granting him a brief respite from the growing chaos outside.

There was barely anywhere to move inside, and he dared not move too much, in case he stumbled into a table or chair, and caused a monumental ruckus that would attract attention. He clutched his gun tightly. The barrel only held four bullets. He had used three already. For what was outside those walls, one was not enough.

He heard a landship drive past, and he managed to catch a glimpse of it through the crack in the wall. It looked like Rommond's driving, leading his assailants in circles, and crushing them when he came back around again. But many of the Iron Guard followed, and they fired all kinds of weapons at the fleeing landship, getting closer with each and every shot.

Then one of the mechanical men halted and turned its head. It had one real eye, and one enhanced by machinery. Both of them now looked at Jacob. Both of them now saw him in his refuge, which offered him no hope at all.

Chapter Twenty-eight

RALLYING CRY

In that moment, as the mechanical man approached, Jacob felt that the city had been all but lost. He did not know what happened in the other quarters, or what happened to the other landships, or what happened to the grounded Skyshaker. All he knew was that he was desperately reaching for his gun.

A hand broke through the wall and seized him, a hand of iron. The fingers worked like pistons, and its grip was tight. The mechanical man grabbed him by the throat, choking him, and hauled him outside, taking half of the wall with him. Jacob instinctively grabbed the metal gauntlet, though he might have been better off grabbing his gun. He felt the life slowly slip away from him, and then the Iron Guard cast him aside, as if it had mercy on him. It did not. It had a gatling gun strapped to its other arm, which it turned to face him.

Then something struck it, and Jacob heard a familiar voice.

"Duck!" Soasa shouted.

Jacob listened, but the Iron Guard did not. Jacob dived for cover just as the dynamite exploded between the mechanical man's feet, tearing it limb from limb, leaving little for a doctor to mend or a mechanic to fix.

"God am I glad to see you," Jacob said as he dusted himself off. He was also glad his reactions were quick.

"Turns out dynamite is just as good as diamonds," she replied.

"If you can get close enough."

"Looks like you got pretty close."

"Yeah, I think I'll stick with bullets." He tapped the barrel. "Though I'm down to one."

"Here," she said, handing him one of her two diamond-loaded guns. "Have one of mine. Besides, I prefer my approach. At least this way we know they're really dead."

She started to run off, but Jacob called her back. "Have you seen Whistler?"

"He's in the inn, the Royal Ribbon."

"A bad time for a drink."

"A bad time for a joke," she said. "Mudro's there too. They're trying to convince the locals to fight. I don't think they're having much luck with that."

"I'll see what I can do."

"Sure," she said, tossing an unlit stick of dynamite up and down in her hand. "I've already seen what I can do."

Jacob followed his old smuggling routes through the city, avoiding the many roads, or the wide streets. He kept to the shadows, but part of him felt like that did not matter any more. The Iron Guard had augmented eyes. They could see in darkness and light.

He found his way to the Royal Ribbon without

confronting anything at all. He sneaked in through the back door, and was almost shot by the nervous innkeeper. There were several people arguing there, including Mudro. Whistler sat despondently in the corner, but he perked up when he saw Jacob.

"Sorry to interrupt an argument, boys," Jacob said, "but the real battle's outside."

"Well, *I'm* not going out there!" the innkeeper cried.

"If we don't fight now," one of the older patrons said, "we'll miss our opportunity."

"The days of the trenches are over, Olly."

"No," Jacob said. "They're just beginning. If you let those creatures mow down the Resistance fighters out there, you'll be fighting at the threshold of your houses. You'll be fighting for each room. These are our trenches, and it's time we go out there and face the enemy, or we'll all be overrun."

"I'm surprised you're banding in with those rebels," the innkeeper said, pointing to his Regime uniform. Jacob had forgotten all about it. With the arrival of the Iron Guard, everyone was essentially wearing the same uniform, with a giant target painted on it.

"Given what we're facing, we've got to band together," Jacob urged. "I don't care if you were born forty years ago or just yesterday. This is your city. This is your home. Those creatures are not your people. One time they might have been. Now they're some mutated, corrupted form. They're the real monsters, and the Iron Emperor doesn't care who they kill. We're all the Resistance now. All of us."

The grumbles were less frequent than they were before, and the rallying cries were more fervent. Several dozen older men seemed primed and ready, even if they were far from their own prime. Perhaps it was because they had less time to live that they were so willing to give up their last days, or perhaps it was because they had families, children and grandchildren, whom they wanted to ensure would live on after them. Some had fought in the old wars, or in the early days of the Great Iron War, and many had a bitter memory of the advancing enemy, and some who manned the Iron Wall had a bitter memory of the Iron Guard.

What was most astonishing to Jacob was that there were demon patrons there too. He only knew it by Whistler's nods and glances. They looked like everyone else, and had differing opinions like everybody else. But many of them were heartened by his words, and many of them cursed the abominations outside, saying the Iron Emperor had gone too far, that he had abandoned sanity, and abandoned all of his people.

How they rallied. How they roared. The sound was stimulating. The feeling was contagious. Who would have thought that the march to death could be made so freely, and with so much feeling, so much vigour? If the battle was right, if the fight was good, then there was a part of every human that could be mustered, and it seemed that even demons had a part like that too.

If the thresholds were the trenches, then the city streets where the no man's land. Men did not walk them. Machine monsters did. Yet the majority of the patrons of the Royal Ribbon made their charge, and even the innkeeper reluctantly went with them, waving his sacred rifle in the air. They all cried out, and the cry passed to other buildings, from which emerged more inspired citizens, more of the home guard to face their iron equivalents.

People with no experience of battle charged with a frenzy at the machine men. They were gunned down by the dozen, but this only angered the crowd even more. The Iron Guard were the elite, but the people of Blackout were plentiful, and there was something that those mechanical soldiers could never replicate: anger.

The people dived at the iron warriors, some dying at their feet, but others knocking the machines from their unstable legs. Hammers and axes fell, breaking parts, bashing steel, cutting wire, and cutting whatever was left of flesh.

As the crowd ran out and overwhelmed the enemy, more people swelled its ranks. Those who watched from their windows could not help but be inspired. They could either fight now when their numbers were many, or they could let the Iron Guard whittle them down, and fight and die when they were few.

Blackout burned anew. As the sun rose further in the sky, the city lit up like a bonfire, the kind the tribes often lit to ward off the spirits of the dead. How many new spirits were created that day, no one knew for sure. All that was known was that humans and demons screamed the same.

Hundreds of civilians died that day, but the Iron Guard had been given orders to put down the Resistance at any costs. They had already ploughed through the people in their way, but they found that more came out to stand there, that more came out to reclaim their city, to fight for freedom, to die that one day their children, human or demon, might live free.

Jacob joined them, killing four of the mechanical men, bringing him back down to a single bullet, a bullet he was reluctant to spend. He kept that gun holstered, and picked up fallen rifles, and here and there a bayonet, which he drove through the heart of a wounded Iron Guard. He severed the wires and broke as much of the machinery as possible, but it always seemed like there was more to break.

The battle raged, and the city burned. As the day wore on, and the sun began to slip from its peak, it seemed to the few remaining Resistance fighters that even if they won this fight, even if they drove back the Iron Guard, they had not really won back the city, for the devastation meant there was little left for them to reclaim.

Rommond was forced to abandon his landship when it ran out of fuel. The furnace gave a final cough, and the steam engine stuttered. The treads ground to a halt, and the general and his gunner quickly vacated it, knowing that the Iron Guard would flock to it, and would finish it off once and for all.

The general joined the growing numbers of civilians, gunning down the machine men, like they had gunned down so many. The angry mob moved from street to street, but Rommond did not follow. He tracked the Iron Guard alone, hoping to take them down one by one, to thin their numbers, until there were no numbers left to thin.

He killed three on his way to the central plaza, where he expected to find the Iron Guard converging. It was eerily quiet. He was not so sure they had been defeated. Perhaps the battle raged elsewhere.

Then he saw a figure stepping around the corner, marching into view, like a contestant entering an arena. The mechanical man, the machine monster, turned on the spot like a turret. The shadows hid its human features, if they were human, but the pipes and wires, the bolts and nuts, were all visible, gleaming in the sunlight.

It had a mask over its mouth, which was tubed to a tank upon its back to let it breathe. Rommond was not entirely sure what gas it inhaled, but he knew it was not just oxygen. His scientists had theorised that it might be some kind of mixture to numb the mind, and numb the pain. It was a man underneath, but the will of the man was pushed so far down that only the monster, only the machine, operated above.

Rommond raised his gun and prepared to fire. He knew how quick they were, how their limbs did not tire like a human's might. Their strength was neither human nor demonic, and it was Brooklyn who once suggested that in the future those two opposing peoples might unite in fear, and see the true iron demons that they had created from their war.

But something held back Rommond's finger on the trigger, like a ghostly hand, urging him to put the gun away. There was no ghost there. He did not believe in them, not like Taberah did, even though he had felt haunted by one for years.

The mechanical man stepped forward, its limbs creaking as it did. The sunlight shone before it like a spotlight positioned by the gods. Rommond did not believe in them either, and yet somehow he felt himself thinking of them, as if he might soon join them wherever they now dwelt, whether it was Heaven or Hell.

Another step, and Rommond still could not fire. The anger leaked out from him, and without that anger, it was as if there was no bullet in the gun. The shadows still veiled the figure, showing only the twisted sculpture the mechanics had made, the augmentations, the "enhancements," everything that any sane civilian would decry as an abomination.

The final step. Rommond knew he had to fire now. It was too close. Its arm was almost raised. What weapons it had, he did not know, but he knew they would be terrible all the same. The mechanical man entered that circle of light upon the ground, that sanctuary from the shadow, and the rays filled every crease and recess, until through the mesh of machinery the man beneath could be gleaned.

Rommond then knew why he could not shoot, and why he would then die that day. He knew that man. He knew those features. He knew that face.

The word fell from his mouth like a bullet casing from a gun.

"Brooklyn."

Chapter Twenty-nine

THE IRON HAND

Rommond stood in horror, his eyes wide, his jaw loose. His hands and knees trembled, and his mind raced, and his heart hammered, and his stomach fluttered. For a moment he lost all sense of self, all sense of his surroundings, and he forget his training, and buried his instincts, until all that seemed to be there, all that seemed to matter, was that mangled figure that stood before him.

Brooklyn. The name repeated in his mind, exploding in his brain, like the bullet some part of him knew he should be firing. It quelled every urge, conquered every thought, until it seemed that it was the only word he knew, the only word he recognised.

Attached to Brooklyn's back was a pack with pistons and pumps, generating a cloud of steam above and around him, but not enough to hide his face, not enough to mask his tanned skin, nor to shroud his faded eyes.

His hair was cut tight, perhaps the greatest offence to the Ootana tribe. At the base of his neck there was a metal plate, in which a tube fed through. It seemed that it might even connect in some way to his brain.

His body was a mix of leather and steel. Most of him was still intact, still more man than machine, but his right hand, the one that Rommond had received in a puzzle box, was replaced with a metal gauntlet. A gatling gun was strapped to his left arm, attached by wires and tubes to the backpack, and clearly as automated as any other part of him.

His eyes were real, but it seemed his spirit was trapped deep inside. To look into them was as if to stare into a mirror. Nothing but the viewer stared back.

"What have they done to you?" Rommond asked, and he felt as if he needed to ask the gods, because surely no human, no angel, no demon could make something like this.

Brooklyn looked at him as if he did not recognise him at all, or, indeed, as if he only recognised him as a target. He slowly raised his left arm, until the gatling gun pointed straight at him. Rommond glared at it, as if he could stare down those bullets, but his glower was more because it was a foreign object, a contraption that made Brooklyn less of who he was.

The general heard a click, and his instincts resurfaced. He dived just in time as a round of bullets blazed in his direction. He rolled into cover, and held on firmly to his gun.

"Stand down!" he shouted. It was an order he had given to his own soldiers, and one he had given to the enemy troops his forces had outnumbered, but never did he think he would have to give it to Brooklyn. For so many years he thought he could never give him anything at all, not even his love.

"Edward Albert Rommond," Brooklyn said, but it was not just his voice. There was a pang of metal to it, as if the machinery had gained the ability to speak. "Target 001. Surrender."

"Never!" Rommond shouted back. At this point he would normally have fired a shot at his assailants. There was nothing like a bullet to show that he would fight until the end. But he found he could not fire. He held the gun close, like he had held Brooklyn's severed hand.

He was still in shock. If that was Brooklyn out there, than what was it that he had buried? He was not able to open the last puzzle box the Regime sent. The devices on it were too hard to crack, and even if he could, he could not bear to see any more of Brooklyn's dismembered body parts. They said it was his head, and he believed them. He had no reason not to. They had proven how low they would stoop. Perhaps they knew he would never open the box. Perhaps they knew that it would break him just the same.

"Surrender to the Iron Guard," Brooklyn spoke. "Bow down to the Iron Emperor."

"I'd rather die!" the general boomed.

Brooklyn responded with a sweeping arc of gunfire, which obliterated the surrounding walls, leaving less cover for Rommond to duck behind. He scrambled to a better position, crouching down, ducking out of sight. His gun was still at the ready, but he was not.

Then the bullets stopped, and he heard the iron feet crushing wood and rock, and he knew that if he had been out there, they would have crushed bone as well. The sound frightened him, but whatever it was about them that frightened his heart and mind, it was Brooklyn that frightened his soul, that made him worry that maybe even one day he too would serve the Regime.

What do I do? he thought, but he knew the answer to his question. *Fight.* Yet he could not fight. *Hide.* Yet the places to hide were dwindling fast. *Flee.* Yet where would he run, and could he ever escape what he had just seen? Could he ever escape the memory of the machine man that was once the man he loved?

Brooklyn scoured the area, lifting up debris that would have been too heavy for him in the past. The pumps continued to pour out smoke, a personal smog, and he wandered through the rubble like a moving city, a little Blackout of his own. How Rommond wished the smoke hid Brooklyn completely from sight. How he wished he could not see.

Then he saw something else. Standing across the street, gun raised, was Soasa, as rough as she had ever looked, her short brown hair unkempt, her clothes grey with dust, her eyes dark and grim.

"No!" the general cried, as he heard the trigger of her gun. He charged out towards her, knocking her down in time to avoid Brooklyn's answering round. Yet he knew he was not trying to save her; he was trying to save Brooklyn instead.

He turned as he heard the diamond bullet strike Brooklyn in the arm, severing one of the cables connecting the gatling gun. Brooklyn faltered for a moment, and it seemed that he was leaking oil and blood. He looked up, confused.

"Get off me!" Soasa cried, pushing Rommond aside. She reached for her gun, but Rommond seized it from her.

"No!" he said. "Do you not recognise him? Do you not see?"

She turned her hardened gaze upon the man, but all she saw was a machine. She knew Brooklyn, but she did not know him like Rommond did. She did not know the creases on his skin, the little blemishes, the tiny idiosyncrasies that mapped his face.

"It's Brooklyn!" Rommond bellowed.

She looked again, but clearly she did not see it. "Are you mad?" she asked. "That's not him."

"It is," the general replied, nodding firmly, and holding her arm to stop it reaching for the gun. "It's Brooklyn. I'm telling you, it's him."

"If that's his body, Rommond, that's all it is. It's not Brooklyn any more."

Rommond looked at the man, who was attempting to repair his arm. All Rommond could think of was Brooklyn working on his machines, on the landships, on the Hopebreaker and the Lifemaker, on everything the Resistance had used to date. God only knew what the Regime had him working on, before they had him working on himself, on the ultimate machine called man.

"Do you not see it?" Rommond asked, and he felt the waver in his voice. "That's him. It's—"

But a hail of bullets stole his voice. A group of civilians, armed with the fallen guns of the Regime, and empowered by Jacob's rallying words, charged into the square, firing as they went. The bullets went everywhere, almost into Rommond and Soasa, almost into themselves. They struck Brooklyn, mostly out of luck, or sheer mathematical probability, for the frenzied mob fired everything they had, hoping to mow down the mechanised man that stood like a sentinel in the centre of the square.

But the bullets that struck him, struck the metal casing, and though a few wires and tubes were severed, they only slowed him—they did not stop him. He turned his iron gaze upon them, just as their bullets ran out, and then turned the newly-repaired gatling gun on them, with ammunition that seemed would never be depleted.

The civilians fell, not one by one, but dozens at a time. Their stolen guns returned to the ground where they had found them, and their blood joined the blood of Regime soldiers that already coated the cracked and weathered paving.

The bullets ceased, and the barrel of the gatling gun slowed its spinning. Then he turned again to Rommond and Soasa, who dived in opposite directions as the bullets sprang anew.

"Do *you* not see?" Soasa shouted to the general. "He's not a man any more, Rommond. Look at what he did to those people. Brooklyn wasn't like that. He made tools of war. He wasn't one himself."

She took a stick of dynamite from her belt, and he knew instantly what she was considering. *She'll never make it*, he thought. *She'll never get to him in time*. What he did not know was if she would fall to Brooklyn's gun, or his own.

"Either you end this now, Rommond," she shouted, "or I will."

Then they both saw another figure on the opposite side of the square, emerging from the haze. It was Jacob, and he had another diamond-loaded gun. He ducked behind cover before Brooklyn could see him, but the general had seen him, and knew what that gun could do.

Jacob hid behind an upturned truck, just in time to avoid the mechanical man's probing eyes. He looked just like the rest, steam for breath, pistons for limbs, wires for arteries, and oil for blood. It was hard to tell where the man ended and the machine began. He shivered at the thought of what it must have been like, and if that part of the creature that was still man was aware, if it knew what it was doing, and if it complied willingly all the same.

Jacob had seen Rommond and Soasa before he ducked for cover. They appeared to be arguing, but it was not clear what it was about. *Perhaps they're fighting over who gets to make the kill*, Jacob mused. For him, he think he would have said, "You go first."

He felt the gun in his hands, larger than a normal pistol, with all of those extra bits and pieces that Rommond had assembled. It was an ugly form, an obvious makeshift design, that betrayed that Rommond had little of the skill that Brooklyn had. The latter, though Jacob had never met him, clearly had a way of finding the beauty in the inanimate, though from what the general had told Jacob, it seemed that Brooklyn would have found something animate in it too.

Jacob peered over the edge of one of the truck's wheels. The machine man appeared to be repairing itself. Across the way, Rommond and Soasa continued to argue, but this time he was holding her back.

And they say chivalry is dead, Jacob thought.

He looked at the Iron Guard once more, wrench in hand, repairing itself like a mechanic might repair a vehicle. It was not normal. It was not natural. This made it a fitting guardian for the Iron Emperor, and a fitting means to wrestle control of Blackout from the Resistance, and crush the dwindling rebels once and for all.

I guess this is my moment then, Jacob pondered. He knew he had to act, while Rommond and Soasa seemed so preoccupied. If that creature finished its repairs, it would be the end of them. The gatling gun span and stopped intermittently. In time it would spin much longer, and when it stopped, all of them would be dead.

Jacob flicked the safety off and stepped out from behind the truck. The mechanical man caught sight of him and gave him a passing glance, before returning his focus to the work at hand. Jacob raised the gun, but knew he was too far away to get a good shot. There was only one diamond-encrusted bullet in that ammunition tray, only a single payout left. Jacob was a gambler, but he was down to a single chip. No matter what he did now, he was going all in.

He stepped closer to the villain, to the wired monster. *Still too far*, he thought. *Just ... one ... more ... step.*

"No!" Rommond cried out, with an anguish that was an ammunition of its own.

Jacob felt his heart slow, his breath stop. Time seemed to crumble away into nothing, so that every moment lasted a lifetime, and the lifetime of all was there for everyone to see.

From his peripheral vision he saw Soasa break free of the general's grip. She reached with one hand for a stick of dynamite as she ran, and with the other for a match. She struck it off the back of her head, where the hair was short and rough, and the match ignited. The fire seemed so much more powerful in that moment than it ever did before. It had the power of life and death.

Simultaneously, he heard the click of the gatling gun's barrel, and then the strike of the spanner on the concrete ground. He turned his head but an inch, just enough to see the mechanical man turning its own head just one inch more, just enough to lock them in its vision. Jacob's gun was raised, and the Iron Guard's was now raising.

The general let out a ferocious roar, which drowned out the sound of the hissing fuse of the dynamite in Soasa's hand, but would not drown out the roar of the explosion that would follow. Jacob joined the aural war with the firing of his gun, a single drum beat followed by the many beats of the Iron Guard's gatling gun.

The bullet of Jacob's gun began its course for the mechanical man's head, while the never-ending stream of bullets from the creature's gun hurried towards the charging woman with her swiftly-ending charge. Those pellets stuck her first, puncturing her torso, but the force of her sprint urged her forward, into more bullets, and, she hoped, into the Iron Guard as well.

But Jacob's bullet missed its mark, for his aim was rattled by Rommond's cry, and the frenzy that followed. Jacob threw himself to the ground to avoid the iron hail, and then he tried to clamber away to avoid the fiery storm that would soon follow.

In his retreat, he saw Rommond racing up after Soasa, but the bullets felled her, and Jacob watched in disbelief as the general ran straight past her and dived into the mechanical man, knocking it from its feet, and rolling with it down the mound of debris, and away from the massive explosion that soon followed.

Chapter Thirty

DYNAMITE

Jacob kept his head down until the ringing in his ears subsided. When he looked up, the dust was thick, masking the debris. He rolled over gently and was relieved to find that the worst of his injuries were a few cuts, scrapes and bruises.

Then he thought of Soasa. He had to find her. He had to see if she was still alive. If the bullets had not gotten her, the bomb surely did. He clambered up and stumbled through the haze. He heard moaning nearby, but it was still difficult to see.

He heard Rommond struggling with the mechanical man. He might have ran to help him, but the general could take care of himself. Soasa was injured, perhaps dead.

And then he found her. He raced towards her blood-soaked body. The parts that were not bloodied were coated in dust. Bricks and rubble surrounded her, with some lodging her in place. She did not move, but she groaned, a weak and fading sound.

"Oh God," she said, when he climbed up to her.

"It's okay," he said. He knew it was very far from okay.

"I can't … feel … oh God." She struggled with the

words, with her breath, with everything.

Jacob tried to remove some of the debris, but then he saw that her legs had been blown off. He closed his eyes and looked away. He could not tell her. He could not show her. He left the rubble there, hiding the wounds.

"Jacob," she said, but it was just another struggle.

"Yes. I'm here."

"I'm dying, Jacob."

He bit his lip, to stop it from trembling.

She tried to reach her hand up to him, but she did not have the strength. "I'm fading," she said. "Guess I get to retire early."

"You can still make it," he said. But he knew that she could not.

"I never got to ..."

"Never got to what?"

"Never got to tell her."

"Tell who? Tell her what?"

"Taberah," she said, and she smiled. "The only woman I ever loved."

Jacob forced a smile, and grabbed her hand, that weak and bloodied hand.

"Do you want me to tell her now?" he asked.

"No," she said, spluttering blood. "I wasn't brave enough. I lost my chance."

"You didn't lose it. I can tell her."

"No. It's better if she doesn't know. It was always ... unrequited."

Jacob did not know what to say. It seemed that his own feelings for Taberah were largely unrequited, and he felt guilty for even thinking this, for thinking of his own needs instead of Soasa's. He focused his attention on her, and found that she was also losing focus.

Then Jacob felt a hand upon his shoulder. For a moment he thought it was Rommond's, but it was too soft, too gentle. He turned and saw the Regime nurse, who knelt down beside him. She did not say a word, and he had few words left inside him to say. She inspected Soasa's wounds, and he looked to her with pleading eyes, but when she looked back, and gave a slight shake of her head, he knew that there was no saving Soasa.

The nurse did all she could, which was not much. She gave Soasa several painkillers, and then she produced a syringe full of a deep yellow liquid. Jacob did not know much about medicine, but the colour did not seem good. When the nurse administered this drug, Soasa's eyes grew wide.

"I see it," she said.

He shook his head. "See what?"

"I see … the light."

Perhaps it was the sun, which shone directly overhead, as overbearing as it ever was in that desert waste. Perhaps it was the pain or the adrenaline, or the substantial loss of blood, or the drugs that coursed their way through her collapsing veins, creating illusionary glimmers. Or perhaps there really was some other light, some glimmer from the afterlife, like a lighthouse, a beacon to guide the wayward soul to newer lands, to newer shores.

Jacob would never know, for she never spoke again.

He closed her eyes, but he left her smile. He did not know why she smiled. The pain must have consumed her so, that she was delirious. Or maybe when it reached such an extremity, it became like Mudro's favoured pain-numbing leaf.

He found it difficult to look upon her mangled body. She was already half-buried, and soon the other survivors could come to bury the other half.

What a way to go, he thought. Perhaps that is how she wanted it. No dull end. No slow decline. Her death was as explosive as her life. She went out with a bang.

Chapter Thirty-one

TARGET 001

Rommond fought with Brooklyn, and he could almost not believe it. That gentle soul was now rough. That soft voice was now course. The violence of his movements, of his struggle, shocked the general, and forced him to fight back. Brooklyn had been his compliment, his opposite, the other half to make him whole, but now he was an enemy, an opposer, an "other" that made him feel divided more than ever, that made him feel empty inside.

To subdue him, Rommond had to resort to force. He did not use his gun. He did not want to end Brooklyn's life. But he used his fists, and he used his might. He pulled wires from their sockets and bashed Brooklyn's left arm into the ground, until the gatling gun fell off in pieces.

And still Brooklyn fought. A human, even a demon, would have given up by then, would have surrendered, would have begged for mercy. But Rommond was not destroying the parts of Brooklyn that were human, and there was no demon there to destroy, but there was machine, and so the mechanical parts of him fought for survival, until there was little left of them to fight.

Rommond was aware of Jacob and Soasa upon the mound of rubble further up, but he could not look to them, or speak to them. Whatever battles they fought, with life, with death, he fought his own, until his muscles ached, and his mind was overcome with fatigue. What ailed his soul, he did not fully know, for he tried hard to ignore it.

Rommond lay there for what seemed eternity, looking up at the sky, that same sky that Brooklyn looked to, that same sky that Rommond had ruled, had shook, had conquered. How they had fallen, like angels fallen out of grace. The sun still shone, but the dust thrown up by the explosion created many false clouds, which dulled those vibrant rays.

He heard Brooklyn attempting to repair himself, but he did not have the means to make those repairs. Rommond had caused significant damage. Of all the people he thought he could never hurt, Brooklyn was number one. What injury he had caused was only magnified inside his heart.

The battle for Blackout was won, but it had come at a heavy price. Many were dead. Some close friends, close colleagues, even loved ones, had not made it through. That was the cost of war, and though it was a high one to pay, it paled in significance to the alternative of total destruction, of complete eradication.

Rommond ordered the Copper Vixens to take Brooklyn back to the Skyshaker, to see what Mudro could do for his body, and what Alakovi could do for the parts of him that were no longer biological.

Everyone was shocked to hear that Brooklyn was still alive, and then disturbed to find that in that form he was now in, he was barely living.

Rommond paid his respects to Soasa, and apologised for not saving her, for choosing Brooklyn instead. Jacob knew that if she could hear his words, she would understand.

The day passed slowly. It was not a day of victory, though the historians would in future times claim it was. It was a day of mourning. It was a day dedicated solely to the dead. The city's streets were filled with them. What losses the Resistance faced were multiplied exponentially by the citizens. Jacob almost wished he had not rallied them, and yet he knew that if he had not, he and they would all be dead.

Night came, but no one slept. The battle continued in their minds, slaying sleep. Jacob found Rommond alone around a campfire, creating little people out of straw, and then casting them into the fire.

"Resorting to witchcraft?" he asked as he sat down beside the general. He took up one of the figures and span it by the arms between his fingers.

"This is an ancient custom of the Ootana tribe," Rommond revealed. "They make a little straw man for everyone who died, and throw it in the fire. It helps them find their way into the afterlife, into the place of their ancestors."

"Do you believe that?"

"I don't know what I believe," Rommond said with a sigh. "I believed in science. Progress was my god. All those vehicles, the Hopebreaker, the

Lifemaker, the Skyshaker, they were my churches, my sacred places, my holy ground. The machinery was my altar, the wires and cables my rosary beads. But look at Brooklyn. Look at what he has become. *That* is the product of science. Religion has its own gods and devils, and it seems that science has the same."

"Because it's touched by human hands," Jacob said. "There's good and evil in anything we do. Maybe that's the great mystery. There are no blacks or whites, just different shades of grey."

Rommond tossed another straw figure into the fire, another little being of his creation, another little life lost in the Great Iron War. "I used to argue with Brooklyn about his beliefs. I used to doubt him, and I tried to force him to doubt. But he was unshakeable. He told me that he did not just believe—he knew. He had a knowledge that I never had, a kind that science, that rationalism, could never replicate."

"Maybe it's good that we don't all agree," Jacob mused. "Life would be very boring otherwise."

Rommond forced a smile.

"How did you meet him?" Jacob asked.

Rommond fixed his eyes upon the fire as he reminisced. "We met about six months into the war, when we tried to get the Free Tribes to join the fight. He's an Ootan, a member of the Ootana tribe. His real name, or his old name I should say, was Kia-ooba-lukassa, and his tribe is one of the friendlier ones, gaining pleasure through offering gifts to strangers."

"Wish I'd known them," Jacob said. "I'm always partial to gifts."

"My truck broke down, and Brooklyn was sent to

fix it," Rommond continued, his eyes unwavering, as if he saw the memories with the souls burning in the fire. "We were amazed at what he could do, with so few tools, so few supplies. We thought we were stuck in the desert, but he got us back up and running in less than an hour. I gave him my pocket knife as a token thank you, a little tool to add to his meagre collection, and he was very gracious, as if I had given him a chest of gold. He gave me a Tamba-runga in return, the feather of a Tamba bird, which the Ootana use to symbolise peace. I thought they meant that they would never join the fight, that they opposed the war, but I found out later that it meant peace between us and them, between me and him."

"If only the Iron Emperor did the same," Jacob commented.

Rommond grumbled. "That will never happen."

"So, not meaning to pry or anything, but how did you know that it was more than just a friendship?"

Rommond smiled. "We went back many times, exchanging supplies, exchanging gifts. Our real hope was to win them over, and use them as a means to win over the less amenable tribes. They clearly did not see our ulterior motive, and Brooklyn least of all. He had a kind of naivety, a bit like Brogan. But he had a deeper wisdom that I couldn't see. I can see it now.

"We walked for hours when others retired to bed. There was some kind of connection there that I could not explain. He clearly felt it too. One night he gave me a Kata-runga, an ornate necklace that symbolises union. I thought it was too much, a gift I could not take, so I offered it back. Little did I know that to offer a Kata-runga back is perceived among the Ootana as gifting union in return, and I had unwittingly agreed to a marriage proposal. Before I knew it, I was being showered in other gifts by the tribesmen. I tried to explain that it was a misunderstanding. I tried to tell myself that I had no time for romance, that I had no place for love. But Brooklyn won me over. Whatever war was going on inside me, he conquered that with peace. He united the broken parts of me. He made me whole for the first time in my life.

"We were wedded then, on the Ootana's sacred ground, but there were some among their people who opposed marriage to outsiders, who thought that it sullied the purity of their people. On the wedding night, they tried to force a coup, but they were driven out, and they became the Anganda, a new tribe that opposed everything we did. They were the reason Brooklyn was captured many years later. They were the reason he's like this now. They hated him not just for his love for me, but for his love of mechanics, of fixing things, of creating things, for his communion with the machine spirits, which they called the Machine Menace. They said that is why the demons came, that Brooklyn had summoned them with his unnatural acts. They wanted to sacrifice him. They thought that that would close the Rift, that it would seal that portal in the sky through which the demons and the sands came."

"Hell," Jacob said. "That's heavy stuff."

"While you were off smuggling amulets, doing Taberah's dirty work, we were fighting on every front, even against people who should have been our allies.

Some wanted to capture Brooklyn for his skills, for his gift, but others just wanted to kill him. God only knows what the Regime did to him, what torture he was put through. They got some of our designs. I'd like to think it was from spies, but I cannot rule out that they forced them from him. Perhaps they had him working on some of their own vehicles and vessels. It is difficult to think about."

"If he's that valuable, then why send him here?" Jacob wondered.

"Because they knew what it would do to me, what it's still doing. Everyone has a weakness, Jacob. They knew mine. They exploited mine."

"Are you sure you want to look at love as a weakness?"

"In war, everything's a weakness."

"Even strength?"

Rommond grumbled. "They wanted me gone. Target 001. I've been fighting them from the start. They killed most of the other generals. But *my* strength came from Brooklyn. He was the man behind the man. For so long I could not get over him, and when it seemed that I was finally making some progress, when I was beginning to get my stride back, they knew there was one weapon that is better than guns."

"Love?"

"They tried to break me," Rommond said. "They tried to shake me."

"Are you broken?"

"No," the general replied. "But I *am* shaken. Whatever my airship did to the sky, the Regime has done to my heart. And what can support it? There are no balloons to hold up a sinking heart."

"But you have him back now."

"I'm not so sure, Jacob. It's his body, or bits of it, but … I don't know what they did to him. I don't know how much of him, if anything, is left."

"Maybe I can help," a voice came from behind them. They turned to find the nurse there. They did not know how long she had been listening.

"I'm not letting you anywhere near him!" Rommond shouted. He stood up and pointed an accusatory finger. "You're the reason he's like this. It's your kind that did this to him!"

"I merely—"

"You merely *ruined* him!" He cast the last remaining straw figures into the fire, which lapped them up, which flickered with the feast, and then he stormed off, clenching his fists.

"Is he always like that?" the nurse asked as she sat down.

"I couldn't blame him," Jacob said.

"Well, I can. I didn't hurt his friend. All I've ever done is try to save people."

"People?"

"Yes, people. Whatever you are and whatever we are."

"Humans and demons, in that order, apparently."

"Apparently," the nurse said. "You don't believe it then?"

"I have my doubts."

"You know, they—*we*—call you demons too."

"I'm not surprised, but what we do is not

demonic."

"Some of you do very evil things."

Jacob nodded. "I suppose you're right."

She extended her hand. "Lorelai Gandergale," she said.

He shook it gently. "Jacob."

"Just Jacob?"

"Well," he said. "I don't know how just I am."

She giggled. "Do you not have a family name?"

"Black," he said reluctantly. "Jacob Black."

"Interesting," she said. "I thought you didn't believe in blacks or whites?"

He smiled at her.

"I'm glad to see a smile," she said. "All those frowns and grimaces are very wearying."

"You've got that right."

She glanced at his arm, then grabbed it. "Who did these stitches? They're a mess!"

"Doctor Mudro. They seem to do the trick."

"The trick?" she asked. "Indeed, if you want nasty scars."

"At this stage I consider them war medals."

"Honestly, I cannot believe a doctor did these. They're the work of an amateur."

Jacob grinned. "Well, he was a magician before."

"A magician?"

"Card tricks and all."

"That explains it then."

"You should see Rommond's wounds," Jacob said.

She sunk her head. "I would, if he'd let me anywhere near them. I can tell he has a lot of scars beneath that uniform."

"He sews himself up."

"God, he probably does an even worse job than your doctor then."

"Well, he's still alive."

She smiled. "That's all any of us can really ask for, isn't it?"

Rommond visited Brooklyn in the Skyshaker, which was still grounded. He was tied down to a bed. It was difficult to see him like that, but Mudro assured the general that it was for Brooklyn's safety, as well as everyone else's.

"Can you hear me?" Rommond asked him.

Brooklyn looked up. There were tears in his eyes.

"We removed what we could," the general said, "but some of it is in too deep. We don't have the doctors we used to have. Much has changed. We've lost so many."

Brooklyn did not respond. He was always stoic, but the silence now was different. Perhaps without the machinery in him, he no longer had a voice.

"What did they do to you?" the general asked. Somehow it felt like an interrogation. Maybe it was the silence. Maybe it was because only days previously Brooklyn had been fighting on the enemy's side.

"I thought you were dead," Rommond revealed. "I really believed it. I felt our connection sever, though I tried desperately to keep it alive. Maybe it was all those bits they put inside you, all those wires, all those drugs. They told me you were dead, and I believed them." He turned away and shook his head. "I shouldn't have believed them."

He paced the room back and forth, running his fingers violently through his hair, aggressively massaging his scalp, as if that might somehow put his thoughts in order, or calm his racing mind.

"Will you say nothing?" he asked. He wondered if he had anything to say.

He left the room, frustrated. He should have been happy, he told himself. He should have felt relieved. Brooklyn was still alive, but somehow it seemed worse than death.

Lorelai, with Jacob's help, petitioned the general many times to let her work on Brooklyn, but it took much convincing just to arrange an audience.

"I can help, Rommond," she said.

He looked at her with forlorn eyes. "How?"

"I worked with several doctors who were employed on Project Ironbreath. I know enough about the procedures they used to make a reasonable effort at removing some of the … additions."

"I don't want your *reasonable effort*," Rommond growled. "Doctors like you are the reason he's not Brooklyn any more. They *changed* him, like an engineer changes parts in a vehicle. They might have wanted him to breathe with iron, but when I look at him now I'm not sure he is breathing at all."

"You have every right to hate those who did this to him," she said. "And I would hate them too, if hate helped. But it doesn't. And I took a vow to help, wherever I can, whomever I can. Right now I can help Brooklyn. I can help restore him. I can help make him Brooklyn again. Will you not let me try?"

Rommond was silent for a time. Who knew what went on in his head? Could he acquiesce to her request? Could he put Brooklyn's fate once more in the hands of the Regime? When Brooklyn had been taken, he did nothing. Could he really do nothing again?

When eventually Rommond made his decision, he did not speak. He simply looked at the nurse, deep into her eyes, and nodded. There was defeat in that nod, but there was also a tiny sliver of hope, buried deep beneath the pain. He walked off, and he forced his chin up, partly out of habit, out of military discipline, and partly in defiance of those who would see him crumble, and use Brooklyn to shake his foundations.

Lorelai got to work almost immediately, for she knew that her old colleagues had made advances she was not present for, but most of all she knew that the longer the implants stayed inside Brooklyn, the less chance she would have of removing them. She only hoped that with them she would not also remove whatever made him the pillar which Rommond leaned upon.

Chapter Thirty-two

UNPLUGGED

Lorelai established a makeshift hospital tent in the city's central plaza, where the wounded were delivered by the truckload. The dead were brought to the desert outside, where they were buried, deeper than six feet, for fear the wind would shift the sand and expose their bones again.

It took two full days of almost restless operations for Lorelai to undo much of what had been done to Brooklyn. She could mend some of the scars of the body, but not the ones of the mind. Those she left to the spirits he believed in. She did not believe in them, but she hoped that if they did exist, they would make him whole again.

Jacob found the body of his father in the city's ruins. It was not clear how he died, but Jacob assumed it was the Iron Guard. He tried to tell himself that it did not matter, that his father meant nothing to him in life, and could mean nothing more in death. But his heart panged.

His father was no angel, but he was no demon either. He had made many mistakes, but as Jacob looked upon the lifeless body, and saw the features he had inherited—that square chin, that sandy hair—he could not help but think: *So have I.*

He regretted not using his last time with his father more wisely. If he had only known. Maybe it would not have mattered, it would not have changed the past, or changed his feelings, but at least then he could have said goodbye.

Whistler visited Brooklyn as he rested. He had not seen him in over three years, not since his capture. Whistler was just a boy then, not someone on the cusp of manhood. He wondered if Brooklyn would even recognise him. He hardly recognised Brooklyn at all. The passage of time had not changed him; the scientists had. Yet his eyes, those big blue eyes, were still the same.

Brooklyn smiled when he saw him. His smile was also familiar, though there was sadness in it now. "Brogan," he said.

Whistler simpered in response. "Hi."

"You are big now. You grow up fast."

Whistler beamed. "You recover fast."

"We all do, when we know how."

"Can you teach me how?"

"Maybe you teach me."

"What do I have to teach?"

"All have lesson only they teach. I see you already teaching it."

"How?" Whistler asked.

"I see it in people who learn."

"I don't understand."

Brooklyn pointed to Jacob, sitting around a

campfire outside the tent. The only spirits he worked with were those in bottles, but he had himself a séance with them all the same.

"He's my friend," Whistler said.

"Your pupil too."

Whistler looked perturbed.

"You see others," Brooklyn noted, "but you don't hate others."

Whistler pouted. "I'm one of them."

"No, you are unique."

"I'd rather be like everyone else."

"Very boring like that."

Whistler laughed. "I guess."

"He learns from you," Brooklyn said, pointing again to Jacob.

"What is he learning?"

"For much time, people call spirits *others* too," Brooklyn told him. "Some say demons. Some say angels. Some say other names your language has no words for. I am ambassador for them. I stand in middle. Easier to see both sides from there. See more clearly. When only on one side, other side is very blurry. You see this too. I see it in you. This you teach him. We need ambassadors. Why? Because war is for division. Peace is for uniting. If we have no one who unites, then how can we end this war?"

Whistler nodded. It was always how he felt. He was just never brave enough to say it. He never thought his opinion mattered in the great scheme of things, when the schemers were too busy with their own. He always had a voice, a soft voice, a voice that was still in the process of breaking, but he never really thought that anyone was listening. Brooklyn listened, and so, it seemed, Jacob listened too.

"I have gift for you," Brooklyn said.

"For me?"

"For someone unique. No gifts for boring people."

Whistler smiled.

Brooklyn took a tiny, furry ball from the chain about his neck and handed it to Whistler. It was very crude, with little beads for eyes, and felt triangles for teeth.

"What is it?" Whistler asked.

"It is worry eater."

"Thanks," Whistler said, holding it up, until it almost smiled at him. "I can keep it?"

"Bigger boys have bigger worries."

"What about you?"

"Very big boy now. I leave my worries far away. Now I think of other people's worries."

"So I guess you worry about them."

Brooklyn smiled. "Very wise. Even spirits worry. At least that way worry eater will not go hungry."

Rommond waited several days before visiting Brooklyn. He tried to say it was because Brooklyn needed to rest, but really he needed more time to come to terms with things, and to prepare himself for the worst.

"I meant to come earlier," the general said.

"I know."

"I wanted to be here."

"I know."

Rommond sunk his head, but Brooklyn took

his hand. "Nothing down there," he said. "Just feet. Just shoes. Better to look up." He pointed up, where the canopy veiled the heavens. "Sky up there. Very beautiful."

Rommond did not look up, but he raised his eyes to see Brooklyn's face. "I've been up in the sky. I *shook* the sky. But it shook me back."

"Then do to sky what you want sky to do to you."

Rommond forced a smile. "You look well," he said. Much of the machine had been removed, and the man was clearly visible underneath. The short hair suited him, though Rommond knew that Brooklyn would not like it, and would want to grow it long again.

"You look well too," Brooklyn said. "I look deeper though, and you not look so well there."

"I'm better than I was."

"Brogan has big worries. You too. More than is your share."

"A leader takes on the problems of all of those he leads."

"I see many leaders now. Easier to share many burdens."

A tear rolled down Rommond's face. "It has been lonely without you."

"I had much company," Brooklyn said. "Spirits never leave. But I only wanted to hear one voice—my general's. I am glad to hear your voice again."

Rommond smiled and squeezed Brooklyn's hand. "You don't know how happy this makes me feel. I … I was nothing without you. I'm surprised I made it this far these last few years, these last few years alone."

Brooklyn was silent and stoic, but Rommond saw through that outer shell, like he saw through the outer casing of machinery that had surrounded Brooklyn. When Brooklyn was choked up, he did not speak. He kept the sorrow deep inside, to save others from having to feel it with him. But Rommond no longer wanted to escape the pain. So long as they were together, he was sure he could fight it, that they could win.

"I have to ask—"

"I know."

"—what did they do to you?"

Brooklyn was quiet for a moment, and in that time he could not keep Rommond's gaze. The eyes were another way to communicate the sorrow, so he closed them and turned away. Yet he could not keep them closed for long. Whatever he saw when he did, it clearly frightened him. It frightened Rommond too.

Chapter Thirty-three

THE WALL IN THE EAST

The clean-up and rebuilding of Blackout started almost immediately. Militia were put in place, but there were not enough trustworthy people to police the streets. The Resistance had organised themselves to resist, not to rule. Even the Treasury, weakened by the attack, were unable to restore total order. Various claimants came forth, and Rommond was frequently called in to settle disputes, which he settled more often than not by taking out his gun.

Rommond was finally informed about Taberah, and he was crestfallen. Had he not had Brooklyn back, it might have shaken him completely. They consoled one another, and Jacob thought he overheard Taberah's tears one night. What she could not say to him, she said to Rommond. He might have felt rejected by this, but he was just glad that she spoke to someone, that she shared with someone.

Jacob sat with the general and a few of the crew, and he almost felt like he had somehow become part of the inner circle. He remembered his old life, and he did not miss it.

"A lot has changed," Rommond said. "Many have fallen."

Jacob raised his glass. "To those no longer with us." He could not help but think of his own child, snatched by fate. Whatever was demonic in the invaders, there was devilry in nature herself, for such an outcome to be ordained.

Rommond looked at Brooklyn. "To old friends."

"And new ones," Lorelai said, sitting down with them. She had earned a place at the table for her work on Brooklyn, but Rommond grumbled, and cast a distrustful look at her.

"So Blackout is ours again," Jacob said. It felt strange to say it. He had not thought in terms of *ours* or *theirs*, only what was his, and what was not.

"What's left of it," Rommond said. He had been brooding on the fate of the city ever since it had been recaptured, as if there were a thousand little battles still to be fought on every street.

"People will resist," Brooklyn said, his voice soft, contrasting sharply with the mechanical monstrosity he had been previously.

"For some, we are the Regime," Rommond replied. "Our authority will be seen as just as much a vice as that of the Iron Empire. Yet we do not rule as harshly."

"I'm not sure we rule at all," Jacob pointed out, as he surveyed the carnage in the city, and listened to the looting in the nearby streets. "Isn't that the Treasury's job here?"

"We've routed them," the general said, "and those who remain are few, and are not as loyal to the Baroness as they were to the previous Grand Treasurer. We've cost them a pretty penny. It is lucky it did not cost us our lives."

"What next then?" Jacob asked. "Do we try to rebuild here? Fend off another wave of the Iron Guard? Surely they will come in force to retake Blackout."

Rommond looked to Brooklyn, as if for advice. It had been so long since he had received any. For many years he had sought advice from the dead, and the only thing they had to say to him was: *Do not join us.*

"Spirits are more restless than ever," Brooklyn said, looking aside, as if a host of beings sat by his side. "They say balance has changed."

"So it has," Rommond said. "For years we played defensive, holding the demons back, until our front line got pushed further and further into the west, until we no longer had a front line to defend. We lost our capital, but now it is regained. The time for defence is over. Now is the time to attack."

Jacob almost expected to hear a cheer from Taberah, but she was not there. The battle for Blackout had been won, but the battle in her body was lost. Wills were broken, and faith was shaken, and Jacob knew not if she, who helped so many avoid giving birth to demon spawn, could recover from her loss, or if it would consume her, like it had done so in the past.

"Where next then?" Jacob asked.

Rommond led them to the eastern ramparts, where he produced a large, baroque spyglass, and held it up to Jacob's face. "Look over there, to the east."

Jacob looked, but saw little but red desert.

"Strain your eyes," Rommond said. "Don't let the

spyglass do all the work. We've had them enhanced. Brooklyn has increased their magnification quite a bit."

"I see a black dot."

"That *dot* is what we made to hold the demons back. It was our barrier, our barricade, against their sweeping advances. A great railway gun, colossal, like the handgun of a god, so great in fact that it could barely move at all. So we built a track for it, from the northern mountains to the southern sea, and it patrolled that route, and could be brought to any location on that track at great speeds. If they invaded in the north, we'd have the railway gun there swiftly. If they invaded in the south, we'd send it down with haste. A single, monstrous gun, to hold back a multitude of monsters."

I guess it didn't work, Jacob thought. He felt it best not to say it.

"When we lost that weapon," Rommond said, "Blackout's fall was virtually secured. Sure, we dug in deep in our capital, and held them off for weeks, but the railway gun held them off for years. It allowed us to reinforce, and to shore up our other defences, and to research and build new tools and weapons. It was our great dam, holding back the tide, our great wall, keeping the enemy at bay. Now that wall, the Iron Wall, separates the west, where we still resist, from the east, where resistance has been thoroughly crushed, and where the Iron Emperor alone reigns supreme."

The general paused and took a deep breath. "It is time to tear down that wall."

"Sounds like quite a goal."

"We'll do it brick by brick if we have to," Rommond said. "Only, each brick is one of our lives. Yet so long as the Iron Wall still stands, the Iron Emperor still rules, for how can we retake the east if that bastion, a bastion of our own making, stands in our way? It is a wall of iron tracks, and we can try to go up north and bypass it, but they will see us from afar and be waiting for us there, and we can try to go down south and even go by sea, but the railway gun has a vast reach, and they will reach us there. There is only one gate through that wall, and that is the gun itself."

"What did you call it?" Jacob asked.

"What I wanted to do in the sky, I already did on the ground. When the demons advanced on that weapon, we made the earth rock, and ears rend, until we got reports back that many of their armies had been routed. So there was really only one name we could give it, only one title befitting of what it could do, and what it will do again when it is back in our control."

Jacob looked to the general with anticipation, but Rommond kept his eyes fixed firmly in the east. When at least he returned his gaze, his voice was hush, as if the memory of that gigantic barrel, on its enormous frame, hauled on colossal wheels upon a seemingly never-ending track, had all but silenced him. Yet when the words came out, they came like the shells of a railway gun.

"The Landquaker."

About the Author

Dean F. Wilson was born in Dublin, Ireland in 1987. He started writing at age 11, when he began his first (unpublished) novel, entitled *The Power Source*. He won a TAP Educational Award from Trinity College Dublin for an early draft of *The Call of Agon* (then called *Protos Mythos*) in 2001.

He is the author of the *Children of Telm* epic fantasy trilogy and the *Great Iron War* steampunk series.

Dean also works as a journalist, primarily in the field of technology. He has written for *TechEye*, *Thinq*, *V3*, *VR-Zone*, *ITProPortal*, *TechRadar Pro*, and *The Inquirer*.

www.deanfwilson.com